TWO DESPERADOS

TWO DESPERADOS

TEXAS REVIEW PRESS • HUNTSVILLE

stories

Susan Lowell

Library of Congress Cataloging-in-Publication Data

Names: Lowell, Susan, 1950– author.
Title: Two desperados : stories / by Susan Lowell.
Description: Huntsville, Texas : Texas Review Press, [2019] |
Identifiers: LCCN 2019011578 (print) | LCCN 2019014966 (ebook) |
    ISBN 9781680032024 (eBook) | ISBN 9781680031935 |
    ISBN 9781680031935 (pbk. : alk. paper)
Subjects: LCSH: Mexican-American Border Region—Fiction. |
    LCGFT: Short stories.
Classification: LCC PS3562.O892 (ebook) | LCC PS3562.O892 A6 2019
    (print) | DDC 813/.54—dc23
LC record available at https://lccn.loc.gov/2019011578

Cover photo: *Monsoon Poem* by Monty Jackson, Flickr
Photo on page 68 woven by Maria Cruz, photo courtesy of Ross
    Humphreys

For Jim Harrison,
who passed me a torch.

ACKNOWLEDGMENTS

"Welcome to Paradise" appeared in *El Portal* (Fall 2017) and "The Road to Town" in *bosque* (no. 7, 2017). "Ironwork" was anthologized in *Stories Through The Ages—Baby Boomers Plus* (Living Springs Publishers, 2017). An excerpt from "Two Desperados" appeared online in *Best Short Stories from the* Saturday Evening Post *Great American Fiction Contest 2018,* ed. Patrick Perry. "The Frog Prince" was published in *Reed* (no. 151, 2018). "The Maze" was published online in *Sky Island Journal* 6 (Fall 2018). A version of "The Woman Who Loved Trees" was published in the Winter 2019 issue of *The Ocotillo Review*. "El Tigre" appeared in the anthology *Awake in the World, Vol. 2* (Riverfeet Press, 2019).

CONTENTS

Acknowledgments   vi

The Woman Who Loved Trees   1

El Tigre   10

Welcome to Paradise   25

Ironwork   34

Love and Death: Eight Short Short Stories   49

    Wheat Country Weddings   50

    Black Decal   52

    M + N   53

    Getting Hitched   54

    The Carpathian Mountains   55

    Bumper Sticker   61

    Cereus Monstrous   62

    The Maze   67

The Road to Town   69

The Frog Prince   79

Captain Death   101

The Witch of the Stacks   136

Shoot   145

Two Desperados   155

The Woman Who Loved Trees

The fat old poet thudded into his desk chair and wheezed loudly, which triggered convulsions, coughs, and gags, but as he weathered them he diverted himself. It was not that his body was a wreck. No, he was under attack. Some tiny rabid beast was fighting its way out of the poetic thorax.

"Mutant! Spawn!" he spat out between gasps. "Squid! Vulture!"

Someday, somehow, he swore he'd finally cough that goddamn vampire coelacanth up. And he would imprison it (gotcha!) in a jar of formaldehyde on his desk along with his other personal fetishes. There they stood: an unkempt stuffed raven, a moon rock, the fang and claw of a grizzly bear, and a small zigzag nugget of fool's gold.

Gradually he caught his breath and began to identify the early morning birdsong. His winter casita was tucked in a canyon beside one of the few permanent streams on the southern Arizona–Sonora border—a rare live trickle through the desert. Yes, that was a Gambel's quail, squeaking like a rubber band.

A female nude, life-size, rear view, hung on the wall before him. From a small and slightly crooked frame that dangled just below the shapely buttocks a beautiful brunette shot him a sidelong glance.

Once his cough had died away, the poet lit a cigarette and patted about for a pen. Dozens of fresh white Bics and yellow legal pads were regularly provided to him, for he was famous. The word "Nobel" had been mentioned, although for the novels rather than the many volumes of poems. Nevertheless he considered himself first and last a poet.

He was a wild man devoted to routines. A gorger and a guzzler,

1

he was still digesting, so to speak, a gargantuan French lunch that he'd consumed one day last summer.

"Hare," he sometimes reminisced to himself, "yes, in port wine and its own blood, yes, inside a calf's bladder. Château Latour 1989."

But when he was not on a spree, his habit was always to rise at first light and write, then sleep, eat, fill more yellow pages with his hieroglyphic scribbles, nap again, head to the bar at 4:35 except on Sundays, then home for dinner, and so to bed. His best ideas came in dreams, and nowadays he napped so much that brilliant notions were stacked up overhead in widening circles waiting to land.

Today's idea, however, was an old one. Taking up a virgin tablet he scrawled: "The Woman Who Loved Trees." Today at last he would write those words. She would never mind.

> *The girl with the green skirt and the sun-brown legs*
> *moves in caution and reverence*
> *as if entering the bedroom of her lover*

Here the poet was seized by a second coughing spell so long and so loud that the dog lifted her hot head from his foot and stared, concerned.

"What? It's nothing!" The paroxysm finally petered out. "Nothing. Failed exorcism. Lie down!" he growled.

He claimed he spoke dog language imperfectly since he was a mongrel (only part dog), but she seemed to understand and calmly dropped her head upon his shoe again.

> *lays her warm palm upon cardboard flesh*

The old man lit another cigarette. American Spirit was his brand, although he didn't actually believe they were more natural or less toxic than others. After everything he'd suffered, capped off by chronic shingles, what difference could any puny carcinogen possibly make? Or, for that matter, a sweet soupçon of poached eel with chicken testicles in tarragon butter?

>*My crazy carcass suppurates, toothless, blind,*
>*its bones burned but not quite dead*

His great subject was himself. Every wall in the house, including the one over the toilet, featured pictures of himself posing with naked showgirls, Beat poets, movie stars, celebrity chefs, presidents, dogs, horses, food, or fish. For years now, sated with fame, he'd refused to accept any more awards. Why, wondered the old poet, were honorary plaques always so heavy, so ugly? What good were they at all? Unlike money they could not be turned into wine, women, and pork. Unlike certificates they wouldn't even burn. They really should be hauled straight to the place his Hispanic neighbors called *el dompe*. No. No more!

In a snapshot taken on a cold day at Wordsworth's grave— so much cleaner than poor Keats's, which reeked unromantically of cat piss—the same exquisite dark-eyed brunette stood some distance behind the living poet. He thought the photographer must have caught her off-guard because that tragedy mask was . . . uncharacteristic.

She faced him yet again across the desktop, her black-and-white eyes like real marble marbles set in a heart-shaped teenage face. Perfectly composed, she raised a knife above what surely was the smallest wedding cake ever cut.

>*still the very me that crashed down on you*
>*breaking the rose-colored apple branches.*

He stopped to stub out one cigarette and light another. No need to smoke outdoors. Not now. Fuming steadily from nose and mouth, he wrote another four lines.

> *Rock rooted elders*
> *talk truth in tissue paper voices:*
> *no hunk of cellulose ever wracked*
> *a human heart.*

He reread the words he'd written so far that morning. Ow! Doubt pinched him sharply. Was this poem—poim as he pronounced it in the Midwestern country dialect of his youth—going anywhere at all? Didn't it sound like a bad pastiche of his own old stuff? Ah, here came the black butterflies. How they loved to swarm inside his skull. Once he'd mentioned the black butterflies to a young woman whose skinny arm he was caressing all the way up to her elbow-knobs, only to recoil when she snatched it away and hissed: "That's not strong enough!"

Perhaps he would have to call his mind doctor. Perhaps it was time for a nap. He crawled onto the narrow bed beside the desk and curled his huge belly-body into the fetal position. He consoled himself to sleep by imagining Montrachet 1989.

The summer that he didn't die, he'd lain in that position for days, delirious, shaking, furious with anger and withdrawal. Surgery had failed him. He knew vodka would not, yet they had taken his vodka away. And as for cocaine . . . ! There was nothing left to do but curse man, woman, and God, and die. Surrounded by a cloud of fireflies, his wife wept, and the faces of friends and strangers darted in and out of his vision like fish across a diver's mask.

"I really don't care if I live or die."

He must've spoken out loud because his wife returned fire: "There's worse than death, you know."

Finally, something besides his own pain seeped into his brain. A man's voice was reading aloud. He even recognized certain phrases: "No, not, go not to Lethe. . . ." and "Beauty that must die. . . ." He opened his one good eye. There sat his worst friend, long estranged except for the letters they exchanged, who in this crisis had driven across the state of Montana armed with Keats's odes.

"Veil'd Melancholy!" His beloved enemy knew how to coax each succulent vowel and consonant from those two words.

"None save him whose strenuous tongue," he chanted, "can burst Joy's grape against his palate fine. . . ." The poet listened and didn't die.

He still wished he could make a pilgrimage to Rumi's splendid turquoise tower in Anatolia, where the occasion of Rumi's mystical death was known as his wedding day. Yet Rumi had advised his disciples to elevate their spirits to treetops, not grandiose rooftops. Rumi must have been a sort of Sufi rapper, forever spouting thousands upon thousands of lines. Me too, the poet thought sadly: too much, too much, too much. Like Simenon, he would like to be able to be silent. And, like Simenon, he thought that if he stopped writing, he would die.

Appetites remained. And satisfying them was, for him, entirely equivalent to Rumi's mystical ecstasy. I too have my religion, he thought proudly. Poims. Girls. Lardo. Vodka, Côtes-du-Rhône, and black truffles. He appreciated Colette's belief that one should eat truffles only when one could cook them by the kilo like mushrooms in butter and red wine and utterly stuff oneself, but in truth he'd never resisted any truffle at all.

The tomb of another of his heroes was more accessible to the elderly and obese. Even better, it meant a trip to France.

While his brother Manuel composed a poem to Franco's sword, Antonio Machado and their feeble mother stumbled across the border from Spain to France, just ahead of the Fascists but also just ahead of "the day of the ultimate voyage" for both of them. Someone had painted Machado's valediction on the tablet at the foot of his grave. "You'll find me on board," it promised, "traveling light, almost naked, like the children of the sea." Subsequent visitors had left pine cones and dry branches, fresh flowers, and a sun-bleached Spanish Republican flag, along with hundreds of personal memorial stones, many weighting down handwritten salutes and messages to the dead poet.

There was also a wishful myth about a lost suitcase full of Machado's poetry, poignant if true because Machado was no Rumi or Wordsworth. His poetic luggage was quite light.

Then, sleep intervened, for the old man suddenly found himself on the bed in his study. He had just tumbled to the surface of a bear dream. Odd! He hadn't dreamed of bears since he stopped eating bear meat many years ago. He was done with killing. His last hunting season had been completely doveless, and although he once had enjoyed chewing on their tiny roasted legs, he now experienced no great regret.

In the distance, cutlery clinked against crockery. For a brief moment the poet's heart raced in desperate hope, and then his housekeeper began to sing of *el amor* and *la muerte* as she set the table for lunch. The capsicum-corn aroma of enchiladas made his mouth water. Propping himself on his Mexican cane, which was gaudy with pink and yellow nudes, he rose, and his pants promptly fell down. Since his body was quite inflexible and had long since lost any semblance of waist or hips, he struggled and sweated to pull them up. Finally, he and the painted ladies set forth, but with every step the pants slipped again.

Beside his plate he found the morning newspaper, and in the middle of the front page he caught sight of a flabby face like a rubber hot-water bottle, half full. He snarled and flipped the paper over.

"Somebody ought to shoot him!"

The housekeeper was a woman whose blubber had settled in concentric rings like a toddler's toy. Once he'd asked her what her Apache and Tarahumara ancestors used to eat for lunch.

At first nonplussed, she finally answered. "Corn?"

Today she carried the steamy, oily casserole to the table, still singing. Suddenly, the poet understood more words, *la pistola* and *la droga*, and he realized that the song she sang was not a ballad of tragic passion but a *narcocorrido*. As he poured himself a tumbler of Châteauneuf-du-Pape he recalled that several members of her family were in prison. He lifted the glass.

"Joy's grape," he said and drank to himself.

Once, he recalled, the highest-priced blonde in Hollywood, luscious as a goose liver, had sat across the table from him and casually plopped an ice cube into the Château d'Yquem he'd poured into her glass.

After another siesta, he returned to his desk, lit an American Spirit, and took up his Bic again.

> *Oh hello, willow oak elm ash cypress yew.*
> *The mad king wished to marry an oak.*

In the middle of the day, the birds fell silent. Perhaps like him they slept, their scaly toes locked onto their roosts in the tall cottonwoods, the velvet mesquites, and the Goodding willows. Sparrows and finches hid in the tangles of the tombstone rose, now a tree itself, which the poet's wife had planted when they first bought the casita on the creek. Wherever they lived, she gardened. First it was vegetables to eke out their macaroni and cheese, and then came the flowers and the groves.

In Michigan, she loved the spruces, white and black, and balsam firs and sugar maples. In Montana, the trees became Ponderosa pines, quaking aspens, junipers, and larches that lived five hundred years. Slow on his feet of late, he'd become, if not a tree lover himself, a stump sitter. There he would sit for half-hours at a time and count, for he was also a counter, the wrinkles in the bark or the fallen leaves. Or the ants, if any. He realized that now he looked a lot like a stump himself, a stout old troll carved out of wood.

"Oh, never mind."

That was what she always said. Breathy from her asthma, she always seemed to say it with a sigh. If he had asked what she meant, she would just have said it again. So long ago and far away, he stopped asking.

Soon enough the time would come to go to the bar, driving illegally because the state had taken his license away. Walking there would be good for him, no doubt, but he could not go so far on foot. He was working on his walking, though. A physical therapist came three times a week to make him do his exercises. She was a handsome muscular black woman, who towered over him, and she was imperturbable even when he asked to see her naked.

"That depends on how you do," she said.

And he was doing better, though she said it wasn't good enough.

He hoped to walk up to a table in France this summer and devour another titanic lunch. First would come a gulp of diamonds: Dom Pérignon 1959. And, finally, thirty-seven courses later, the chocolate cigarettes.

At the bar, his glass of vodka would automatically arrive. Sometimes people came to meet him there, either friends or flatterers who laughed too loud and stayed too long. He would speak lewdly to the homely waitress, who'd heard it all before. Perhaps today he would deeply embarrass her and propose, but what if she accepted? He would smoke and crush out a half a pack of cigarettes. And he would feed little paper cups of sour cream to the cat.

> *At the dog's grave in the woods*
> *you told me go away forever*
> *still I reach for phantom trees in another country.*

He skipped a space. Below his heart the coelacanth gave a sudden shocking wriggle but he told it, "Just you wait!" and wrote on:

> *Lover come bac*————————————————————

The last line traveled straight across the edge of the yellow pad and onto the desk before it stopped.

When the housekeeper returned at five o'clock, she found the poet and the dog together on the floor. The dog lifted her head, but the poet lay as still as a log.

In one hand he clutched a pen, and in the other, a burnt-out cigarette.

El Tigre

Halfway up Skeleton Canyon, Lola struck a fresh cat track.

The trail is solid rock there, so I didn't see a sign of anything. But I trust my dogs one hundred percent, and these were all Walker hounds with big orange spots, hard feet, and good noses. So when Lola busted off towards the north, bugling and baying for all she was worth, I pulled out behind her on my red mule, Colorado, with the other five hounds hollering their heads off all around us.

Finally we hit the top of the ridge, Skeleton's Backbone we call it here in the mountains where Arizona and Mexico come together. There's not a particle of difference in the land, of course. It's rough and parched on both sides of the line. The mountains run north and south across the border just like the plants and animals do, although as you go farther south there's more water and the tropics start creeping in. Then you get to the Sierra Madre. Badland, *malpaís*, whatever you want to call it, every inch of this border country is good to me. I know I'm nothing but a whisker on its chin and I don't want any more than that.

When I looked down from Skeleton's Backbone, there was Lola doubling back toward the south again. The ridge drops off pretty steep there, but I spurred Colorado and he took off like a long-eared hang glider. Each time he hit the rocks with his steel shoes, sparks flew, and about six jumps later we landed at the bottom. That's not the kind of thing a horse can do, which is one reason why I like mules. A mule's eyes are set in his head so's he can see all four of his feet at once and know exactly where he's setting them down, but a horse sees only his two front feet. That's what they say anyway. There are other differences too, of course, a big one being that mules don't tend to spook at the smell of blood or lions the way horses will.

My name is Kendall McDonald, and I don't hunt for no reason or kill for no reason. The name of the game is balance. I never meant to hunt that day at all, just to prowl through some of my cows, check some waters and fences, get a breath of the country, and give the dogs a run. And run they did, so fast that it was hard to keep in hearing distance of them. I know their voices, and Lola never stopped her yodeling. I also clearly heard Dab and Dash, the goofy half-trained two-year-olds. I needed to catch up to the dogs to gather them in again, but a stiff March wind was blowing the sound of their voices away from me and also blowing the cat's scent away from them. I watched for track as I rode along. Finally, the ground became a little softer and soon afterwards I saw the fresh tracks of what I believed to be a big tom mountain lion, and I also smelled skunk. I guessed the lion had recently killed one and eaten it, and the skunk smell was kind of counteracting the effect of the high wind on the dogs' noses.

When I say lion I mean mountain lion. Folks in other places may say cougar or onza or wildcat or puma or panther or catamount or painter or ounce cat or mountain screamer and the list goes on and on, but we just say lion. The lions in our part of the country are tawny like a camel-hair coat or a dry-grass mountainside, where they blend right in, but they don't have manes and they can't roar. At one to two hundred pounds, they're smaller than zoo lions and not always the top predator in their area. They might, for example, lose a matchup with a bear or a wolf pack. A lion is just about the same size as a medium human being, or a deer, which is what they eat whenever they can, unless they develop a taste for colt or calf or alpaca or housecat. Or hiker. Or hunter. There they come up against the highest predator of all, and things can get out of balance. But for now, anyway, mountain lions are not a species at risk. If anything, there are more now than there used to be when I first went hunting.

The six hounds were all together now, running the scent up into Ketchum Canyon, where outlaw gangs used to have their hideouts a hundred years ago. If you look, you will find one of them, by the name of Zwing Grant, who's still there right where the Apaches left him, in his grave. The way the story goes, back in the 1880s a band of Apaches stole some gold from Mexican miners and escaped with it across the border, but then Zwing and his brother stole the gold from the Apaches. But they didn't keep it long. My dad took me past Zwing's rock pile for the first time in 1943, one day when we didn't plan to hunt either because June's just too blasted hot and dry for man or beast. No, June is not a good month to hunt lions. Next thing I knew, though, I was leading my dad's horse through the mesquites and he was off on foot following the hounds.

On this cold March day fifty years later, I didn't stop for old Zwing either. I was busy noticing, in what soft dirt there was, the very large and very round yet short tracks that the cat was leaving behind him. I'd been seeing those tracks in that area from time to time since early the year before, along the ridges and in the canyons where I've lived and ridden and hunted all my life.

Colorado took the trail at a high trot, loping whenever possible. These conditions were so far from ideal that I was surprised the dogs could follow a scent channel at all and push anything along so fast in such dry, windy, rocky, big-bluff country. We went a couple more miles like this, me having my doubts all the while, before we finally came out on the high-rimrock above Sycamore Canyon and I just barely caught the sound of the hounds way off across the basin in some steep tan bluffs on the other side, almost in Mexico.

They were letting out the short choppy barks that tell me they've bayed the lion, either up in a tree or in the rocks.

So Colorado and I plunged down into the canyon toward the place where they seemed to be, but we weren't even half-way down the stickery slope before I could hear that the dogs and the lion were off and running again in yet another direction: east.

"Dang that booger!" I said to myself, or words to that effect. I don't cuss, mostly.

I spurred my good long-legged mule over another ridge and then finally caught sight of the dogs maybe a quarter of a mile away. In spite of that hundred percent trust, I still couldn't believe any lion could run that fast for so long. Maybe the younger hounds had forgotten their job and taken off after a coyote or a deer? I guess it was more like ninety-nine percent trust I was feeling at that moment. I got off Colorado so's I could squat down and take a good look at the nearest tracks, and sure enough they were the long strides of a big cat running fast. They were unusually deep.

"Tom lion all right," I thought, and probably the biggest I'd ever seen.

Some people snicker when I look at a track and say, "Four-year-old female," or whatever it may be. But I don't ever laugh at anybody who's paying me good money to guide them, which I do a lot of. I'm licensed. "Okay," I say to myself, "we'll see." A family cattle ranch is usually a hand-to-mouth business and most of us do more than raise cows to get by, and even though the world has changed, we're still just getting by. I do guide trophy hunters but that's not all. Nowadays my dudes also come looking for rocks, trees, bugs, or lizards, and sometimes movie locations, though since the Western has pretty much gone extinct we don't see much of Hollywood anymore. One guy comes to write wilderness poems and drink Scotch whiskey. I serve them steaks and then we sit on the porch and I play my guitar and tell stories and smile. And listen. There's a whole lot to learn if you have the patience to look for sign, and I'm not just talking about hunting.

To read sign, to catch up with your dogs, or even just to get across a particularly bad patch, you sometimes dismount and lead your mule or your horse, or else tie it up and go on foot or hands and knees because there are some places even a mule can't—or, being a mule, won't—go. Or maybe you hand off the reins to someone else, like my father did to me that day in '43 when his dogs hit on some scent and went to barking and cold trailing a lion running through the brush.

Just like this raw spring day, and most other days of my life, that June one in '43 started hours before sunrise. It's vital to start early in June. The temperature hits the high nineties and the water in the stock tanks dries up, and heat and thirst are killers. But it wasn't the weather that killed the little filly we came upon, ate her heart and guts, and left her disguised with leaves. A lion returns only once to a kill. They like fresh meat.

Today there was no lion kill. Maybe the taste of skunk's a little like hot pepper and leaves you with a glow so you don't feel hungry for a while? At this point the hounds were baying him up in the rocks, but I knew that when he rested he'd slip away through slots and crevices too narrow for the dogs. They'd have to find a way down and around the bluff, and by then he'd have a head start. It would be a game of catch-up again. Would the lion, the dogs, Colorado, or I give out first? But there's nothing like a chase, so on we ran.

"He must be a wild son of a gun!" I thought.

Now they headed for a flat-topped mountain called the Biscuit, running in and out of my hearing even though I tried my darnedest to keep up. They climbed the nearly vertical north side of the Biscuit, and I knew I couldn't get through there with Colorado, so I decided to go rimming to the east, and when I topped out on the spine of the ridge, sure enough, I heard them again on the other side of the Biscuit. This time I also recognized the voices of two older, wiser dogs, Chet and Bee. That was a relief.

So I kept on trotting and watching for fresh hound tracks to follow. I'd gone a mile or two when I heard them "barking bayed," as we call it, again, way below me in a place full of yellow boulders, scrub oak, and piñon pine. Looking down, I saw what I thought was a lion crouched very still on top of a bluff. Sometimes it's hard to tell. Lions don't want to be seen and they are geniuses at hiding. But no matter how many times it's happened to me before, whenever I see a lion my heart goes bang.

I'll never forget my first one. There's no horse on earth that'll pass up a chance to scrape off his rider on a low-hanging branch, preferably a thorny one. Most likely I already knew that in '43 but, if not, I got a good lesson that day. I also knew I must keep moving toward the sound of my father and his dogs, even though on top of everything else his horse was not wholeheartedly inclined to follow me.

Finally, right about sundown, after twelve hours and twenty miles of zigging and zagging, the dogs bayed the lion, and I saw him. My dad shot him with his .22 caliber pistol. In those days, the hide and the skull brought a bounty from the state that was worth a lot to us because we were poor. By the time my dad and I got home, it was midnight and my mouth was so dry I couldn't spit. We'd had no food or drink since breakfast except green water from a cow pond tasting of cow piss. I was six years old.

We hunted together for almost fifty years after that. We guided people from all over the world, including some whose names might surprise you, and treated them all just about the same. At sixty-one, I've seen at least a thousand lions. I've crawled into caves where they lay growling in the dark. I've caught them and shot them and lost them and eaten them and raised them as pets.

I rode Colorado to within fifty yards from the bluff where the big cat sat, tied the mule to a tree, and bushwhacked my way toward the sound of the dogs. When I got clear of the thick brush and looked up, I was stunned by the surprise and beauty of the scene. The cat was large and stocky with a big round head, and he was tawny for sure, but on top of that he was also completely covered with a paw-print pattern of black spots.

"God almighty!" I said out loud. "That's a jaguar!"

He was absolutely beautiful. I'd always wanted to see a jaguar in the wild but never had, except once in a zoo, and that hardly counts. It was sad to see him there: I don't like zoos. Jaguars used to range all the way from deep in South America to the American Southwest, but around here we thought they were gone for good. I'm a licensed guide and I sometimes work for the Game and Fish, so I know the law. They're endangered and protected. Shoot one, go to jail. (Or else shoot, shovel, and shut up, some of my neighbors would say.) But he was ungodly beautiful.

"Kendall McDonald," I said to myself, "you pay attention! This is a once-in-a-lifetime moment."

I felt deeply thankful for it. I just wished my dad was there, first for the chase, and now to see what I was seeing.

The jaguar gazed down at the hounds as they circled and bayed, but he didn't seem to notice me, even when I went scrambling uphill to Colorado. I fumbled in the pouch I carry on my saddle horn and jerked out my camera. Then I tumbled back to the first place I'd seen the jaguar and fired off a shot.

I was afraid it was the only chance I'd get, but after sliding farther downhill I did manage to grab a closer shot.

The jaguar crouched calmly on top of the yellow bluff, not panting at all. Between him and me there were two scraggly piñon pine trees and a steep drop-off. Beyond him lay the spine of another ridge, and beyond that, the blue sky and the purple mountains of Mexico. *Tigre's* what they call a jaguar there, *el tigre*. But this cat seemed more like a leopard than a tiger to me.

He took a look at the dogs, then at me, then at the dogs again. Finally he raised himself on his front legs while still crouched on his haunches, and he stared at me, and I saw in his eyes that he was going to make his move. I've seen that look in the eyes of many a lion just before he jumped out to make another run, or to pounce on prey.

So, when the jaguar pussyfooted over the rock in my direction and gathered himself up, I backed off, snapping pictures as I went, and he just eased off the cliff like a puff of smoke. I hollered at the dogs to come to me, but they'd already seen the cat jump and didn't even hear me. All seven of them vanished together, and the race was on again.

As Colorado and I brought up the rear, I remembered a tom lion I'd seen recently, all scarred up with half his tail bitten off, and now I could guess who'd tangled with him. The jaguar ran half a mile and holed up at the bottom of a chute in a vertical canyon we call the Box. By this time I was very worried about my hounds because jaguars are top predators. They pounce on swimming alligators. They'll carry a cow up a tree and pulverize its bones, or chomp a sea turtle like a cream puff. How was I going to get the dogs off this one? A famous hunter told me once that a jaguar killed seven of his dogs in a single hunt in the mountain and jungle country of the Sierra Madre.

I caught another strong whiff of skunk, and I heard the hoarse roars of the jaguar blending with the crying of the hounds. From the sound of things, there wasn't much time. Now I could see five of the six dogs, Lola, Bee, Dab, Dash, and Pearl, all perched on a ledge, looking down and barking like mad. They had the jaguar at bay.

I knew I shouldn't kill him and the truth is I didn't want to kill him.

But I was scared for my good friends—my dogs. Trying to find Chet, the one dog I couldn't see, I sneaked a peek over the edge. Down in the rocks and shadows the jaguar lay with his head turned away, fixed on something else, probably Chet. I inched closer.

Then the jaguar looked up, and we stared eye to eye again. His eyes were that color that metal turns just before it goes white-hot. Again I watched him calculate and I knew exactly what he was going to do, and the dogs knew, too.

Words are slow. This went fast.

You might say all hell broke loose. The jaguar leapt at me. The hounds jumped between us with Lola in the lead, and the jaguar clawed her in the side of the head and drug her into his hole, and Pearl and Bee flew to help her. While he swatted at them, Lola managed to break loose, but instantly the jaguar caught her again by a hind leg. Then finally Chet popped up at the bottom of the den and attacked from the rear.

Meanwhile, I hollered and grabbed at whatever collars, scruffs, and tails I could reach and tried to drag them away. Almost without thinking I also scooped up handfuls of rocks and dirt and threw them down the hole. That worked! Caught between Chet and the rain of pebbles, the jaguar let Lola go, and I got ahold of her collar and hoisted her away. By now most of the hounds were bleeding. But they'd probably saved my life.

"Give him some air!" I yelled and slapped the dogs back with my hat.

I could see the jaguar was going to jump again. As we all tumbled backwards I raised my right arm and took aim. For a moment we were all safe, and I lowered it, but then those tomfool young hounds Dab and Dash went after him in spite of all my hollering.

No way to stop them, so I checked over the four dogs that were left. To my amazement, the damage was not too bad. Lola's head was all clawed up, and one of the little bones in her left hind leg was broken. Chet, Pearl, and Bee were also clawed, but not much. I tied them up near Colorado, hoping they wouldn't chew through the ropes and follow me, and then I started after Dab and Dash. Luckily, the two goofballs figured out they had no backup and turned back on their own.

The jaguar was gone, except for whatever pictures might be caught inside the camera, and I was pretty doubtful about that. The last we saw of him, he was headed south at a steady pace. He'd find water, greenery, and better pickings in Mexico, I thought, and I wished him good hunting.

I settled Lola across the saddle in front of me and turned Colorado's head toward home. It was the first time I'd ever chased a jaguar but not the first time I'd ever felt like prey. "There's a lot of top predators out there," I reminded myself.

I wondered what to do next. Should I tell anyone? Shouldn't I just shut up? I wished I could talk to my dad. I sure didn't want to bring down any trouble on myself or my neighbors. A hundred miles away in Tucson there's a guy who I think came from Massachusetts or maybe Ireland, and who wants to save the world from people, especially ranchers. He says ranchers have spent centuries destroying the place where they live, so they deserve to be destroyed themselves. And he's not working alone. He's dead serious and has lawyers and money. If they had their druthers, this place would be a jaguar preserve before you could say Jack Robinson, and we'd be in a zoo. Or up in Skeleton Canyon right next to old Zwing, much better than a zoo.

Yet, as we jogged along I couldn't help feeling that the jaguar had laid some kind of hoodoo on me—just happenstance, I knew, because given the opportunity he'd have killed and eaten the dogs and me. We'd surely taste sweeter than skunk.

I thought about land. I thought about sun, rocks, sky, seasons, weather, plants, and animals moving in great cycles all in balance. Then here comes the human race, monkey-wrenching the universe right and left but really just little grains of sand who think they're mountains. Maybe skunks *are* sweeter. It tickled me to think I might agree with that guy in Tucson about some things. Oh, give me dogs and mules any time! I've also known quite a few cows I liked better than people. Animals are far more logical and far less crooked.

I've got neighbors who'd laugh their heads off, or worse, to hear me say this stuff. There's one in particular who claims he owns his ranch down to the center of the earth and up to the top of the sky and nobody can tell him what to do. It's us against them, he shouts, and nobody around here likes to cross him. Most of the women around here hate him but spending your time hating is a lot like cussing, if you ask me. He used to have a wife himself, who disappeared between one Cowbelle club meeting and the next. She went away, he said, but he never said where.

He doesn't think much of women. He can't seem to stop bad-mouthing a young lady who came though here a few years ago, working on a book about cowboys, she said. Sometimes, when we talked to her, her eyes would bulge like a pug dog's, but she seemed nice enough. Then her book came out and it was about cowboys, all right, but it was not so nice. Her title hit her theme right on the head: *Die, Cowboy, Die.* But I say no matter where you look, ma'am, you'll find angels in damn short supply. Take the guy in Tucson. According to what we hear, his war against ranchers is also religious, and it has something to do with that old fairy tale about the prince who was a frog, though I could have this all wrong. They also say he once shoplifted a pair of boots and a pair of bedroom slippers from Walmart and his excuse was that he was desperately poor, though I could have that wrong, too.

When I got them developed, the pictures changed everything. They took my breath away: the dogs, the Biscuit, the oak leaves, that ungodly spotted hide. Those eyes.

"Holy moly," I said.

I began to call some people that I know, including a couple of birdwatchers and a guy who counts weeds. I talked to a lizard fellow and a fish lady. I called a senator or two. I called a fellow who sells fancy fish poles for not catching fish. And then I called the poet.

Of course it was really the jaguar that changed everything. Probably it doesn't hurt that I look the part, being tall, Western, and some say good-looking. I'm not much for meetings and crowds, or fame, though, so sometimes I saddle up Colorado and let the dogs loose and we ride into the mountains just to escape the buzz. But I have to come back to smile for the cameras, just like the jaguar. Lots of cameras. First came the motion-sensing game cameras, and now we're deep into infrared and digital and video and cell and internet, which leads to all sorts of new shenanigans, some okay, some not. Frankly, I don't like publicity. It's not real. It reminds me a little of the old Hollywood Western days. But I've finally got so I can say "charismatic megafauna" three times fast without cracking up, and it's too late to go back now.

Sometimes I let my phone just ring. Sometimes I find myself answering it.

Half a dozen years went by before the guy in Tucson finally called. He'd stuck his finger in a lot more pies by then too.

"Kendall McDonald?"

"Yes."

"Really?"

I told him yes, really.

"This is Piers Piggott from the Native and Nature Foundation."

"I know who you are," I said.

"Right," he said and explained anyway. As I listened I could hear a funny little accent in his voice but couldn't tell if it was Massachusetts or Irish. I wondered what he wanted. By this time he'd outgrown his two-bit outlaw phase. Big lawsuits were his game, especially against cattle, timber, and mining companies, and along with his other donors he'd found a way to make the government to give him money so he could have equal justice. That meant he was always suing the government too. The Native and Nature Foundation had an operating budget of several million dollars a year and, according to the Tucson newspaper, had just spent $1.5 million in cash to buy a mansion for their headquarters. Equal justice is a fine thing, and so, I guess, is power.

I've often thought back to the Wal-Mart hiking boots and bedroom slippers and wondered which pair of shoes Piers Piggott wanted most. Did he start small and get tempted to grab more? Or did he go first for the boots, with the slippers as an afterthought?

So now, I asked myself, is the jaguar the hiking boots or the bedroom slippers?

Finally he got to it: "We need your pictures."

"They've been published," I said. "Can't—"

"Our jaguar team needs really good prints because we need to compare your jaguar to our jaguar. No two have the same pattern of spots, right?"

"That's right," I said. "Are you talking about—"

"Tigre Two," Piers Piggott said impatiently. "We call ours Tigre Two. Probably not the same as yours but we want to be sure."

"The one that was photographed by the game cameras near Patagonia?"

"Right."

"The one that was caught in a trap?"

"Just to install a radio collar so we could track him."

"Baited with female jaguar piss from the Phoenix Zoo?"

"I never authorized that!"

"The same jaguar that was left dangling in the net for days?"

"Our jaguar team had a permit. Everything was perfectly legal."

"The one that died."

"Euthanasia became unavoidable, right?"

"Well," I said, "I'm real happy to tell you that our jaguar team has studied the Patagonia pictures and decided that was a different cat. So—"

"I need proof, right? Not some rancher's . . . word."

I mentioned that we're working with the biologists at the International Jaguar Conservation Project and with some folks down in the Sierra Madre where a healthy population of jaguars is breeding. Everybody feels pretty sure that what we've seen in Arizona are lone males—wanderers from Mexico, outliers. In the silence that followed I decided not to bore him with our other conservation projects. Of course our neighbor from the center of the earth would sooner shoot himself than join us.

Finally, Piers kind of expectorated some words that were

not in my vocabulary and hung up. As I said, I'm not much for cussing, or maybe he was speaking Irish. But nonetheless he surprised me.

"Why Kendall," I said to myself, "I do believe you're a hiking boot."

And the jaguar, and the land? Mere bedroom slippers!

I've never owned any hiking boots. They don't fit through the stirrups on a good red mule. For a moment I wondered if Piers Piggott ever took anything else that didn't belong to him, and just didn't get caught, but then I figured I knew the answer to that. The frog prince is still a mystery to me.

I stood still and listened to the quiet. Quiet isn't that quiet, of course. The wind was whistling and that made the grass hiss, but they weren't loud enough to drown out the slow kra-a-ks of a raven flying by. And then an old saying of my dad's came to mind, so clear I could almost hear his voice: "Sometimes, young lady, in order to stay the same, you've got to change."

Welcome to Paradise

From the top of the big hill you can see the whole desert valley down below. The city that fills it sizzles and glitters through the smog like broken glass in roadside dirt, and at the bottom of the hill lies the corner where the street vendors are.

You call this moment "the drop-off." It reminds you of the first sight of the ocean, and it never fails to add a certain fillip to a dull daily drive. The way down is easy. The car seems to float from the drop-off to a busy crossroads surrounded by scraps of vacant land. It's a perfect site for peddlers.

But on this Arizona August morning there is only one, the old watermelon man. He sits on the tailgate of his pickup truck, wearing a pork-pie hat and swinging his legs. Propped up beside him is a watermelon, split open, and under a make-shift tent of shade cloth, the back of the truck is stacked high with green bombs. A crudely lettered sign reads:

WATER MELONS
CANTS

But there are no cantaloupes. All day long you carry in your mind the vision of that cool rind corseting flesh hot in color, frosty in the mouth. But when you pass by later, you notice that half the seeds are flies. And you do not stop.

In September the sign bus appears. It's a converted school bus containing a family: man, woman, child, and dog. Have they changed since last year? The toddler has grown into a preschooler, but the woman is still a thin blonde, the dog a blotchy mutt with a long tail, and the man a paraplegic in a wheelchair. Inside the bus is a workshop where he makes wooden signs to order. Examples hang from the bumpers, the protruding stop sign, and the windows of the bus:

SIGNS WHILE-U-WAIT
THE BYRD'S NEST
KEEP ON THE GRASS

And, engraved inside a rough heart pierced by an arrow, there is a pair of initials:

K + S

All lines and edges are deliberately uneven. The words appear to be burned into the wood.

Do these people live in the bus? Who knows? Like most of the other vendors who favor this corner, they arrive after the morning rush and leave by dusk. Their hours are longer on weekends. The pace, however, always seems slow. First they park, not too close to the watermelon man, in a favorite spot on a half-acre triangle of dry, scraped earth. They set up the sample signs; the young woman unfolds her lounge chair. As long as summer lasts, she sunbathes in halter tops and short shorts. Meanwhile, the dog and the child roam around the bus, somehow avoiding the traffic, and the man bends over his signs in progress. His straight mouse-brown hair hangs halfway down his back.

The old man continues to offer watermelons, but it is hard to tell if he ever sells one. Placidly, he sips the Big Gulp in his hand and watches the cars go by. On rare occasions a wifely old woman fusses about the truck or hikes to the 7-Eleven store across the way, never sitting down beside him. She's not a peddler at heart.

Now, for the first time, the walker appears. But, judging from the brick face beneath his baseball cap, he's been on the streets for years. A fit, stringy man of about thirty, he walks hard, as though he has a destination and a schedule. He attacks the big hill without pausing. In spite of the lingering heat he always wears an army fatigue jacket. Sometimes he carries a can (Coke? Coors?), sometimes a small brown-paper bag. After you meet him repeatedly at different times, both coming and going, always expressionless, you realize that he walks this route all day.

Other vendors sprout upon the corner from time to time, and sometimes another pedestrian passes by, but the watermelon man, the sign bus, and the walker are the regulars. On September weekends, a family in a truck with Mexican license plates sells green corn for tamales, and now and then a small refrigerator truck also turns up. One side proclaims:

LOBSTER TAILS

The other side retorts:

SHRIMP

Huge scarlet claws dangle on either side of the windshield, while the rest of the plastic beast perches like a gargantuan scorpion upon the roof of the truck. The man behind the wheel never looks up from whatever he is doing in his lap.

One morning, the watermelon man sits petting the dog from the sign bus. The walker swings past, continually tossing and catching a small object as he goes.

The young woman lies sometimes supine, sunglasses facing the sky, and sometimes face down. She wears colors that catch a driver's eye: fuchsia, chartreuse, fluorescent orange, black. Smoke rises from the cigarette she holds at the end of an outstretched arm. Gradually, her skin acquires the look of oiled furniture. Within a few weeks the child is eating watermelon, and the fruit vendor displays a new wooden sign:

A GREEN THOUGHT
IN A GREEN SHADE:

WATERMELONS

About the middle of October there is a transformation in the watermelon man. He fills his truck with pumpkins and lines up a row of jack-o'-lanterns facing the street. They are irresistible. If you stop to buy a pumpkin, you find the old man carving one for the child. Boy or girl? The small white-blond creature wears a T-shirt that says "SEATTLE." Now the young woman strolls over to see the finished jack-o'-lantern.

"Cute, Frank," she tells the old man. Up close, the tufts of her hair are blond at the roots but dark at the ends. The child pokes a finger through the pumpkin's eye. You choose a large coppery, warty spheroid and ask the price, for nothing is marked.

The old man considers. "Four dollars."

The young woman pays no attention to the child as it lugs the jack-o'-lantern away. Even though the wind is cool at the end of the day, stirring together the odors of car exhaust and raw pumpkin, her mahogany midriff is bare. She stares into the traffic as it butts through the intersection.

On impulse you add a second, smaller pumpkin.

"No charge," says the old man.

He places the pumpkins snugly together on the floor of your car. The skin on his fingers is cracked and dusty.

"Punkins'll ride safe there," he remarks.

As you drive away you see a new sign hanging from the bus:

WELCOME TO PARADISE

And the black letters are not burned into the wood after all. They are merely painted on it.

A few days later a large truck thrusts itself between the old man and the sign bus and disgorges a mountain of pumpkins. The old man tries to compete for a few days, then disappears until Halloween is past. Once you see the blonde sitting with the new pumpkin sellers as you go by. Late on Halloween night the corner is deserted and dark except for one small flickering gray light.

November brings chiles in heavy, rubbery, peppery strings like red leather icicles. The watermelon man hangs them all around the outside of his truck. And November brings another vendor. Every day this new man spends a long time setting up his display of artificial woolly seat covers, which flutter from a clothesline in front of his van, and also miniature windmills, which spin busily together on the ground. You do not know the term for the other dizzy devices that twirl on the clothesline beside the seat covers.

But soon he posts two new wooden signs:

SHEEPS KIN, $20
WIND SCREWS

The smog is worse in winter. Year by year the ugly city fills up the valley below until the view from the drop-off is nearly smudged out. The surrounding mountains seem to grow hazier every day. But it's possible to pick out the walker's silhouette far down the street, heading south. At the corner, the wind-screw man watches a woman in taut pink jogging tights as she runs north.

In the first week of December, a Christmas tree lot appears at the intersection. Unlike the other street vendors, the tree sellers also do business at night under a string of white-hot lights, and they live in a trailer at the back of their little temporary forest. After midnight they lock up the trees inside a portable chain link fence.

Where do the others go at night? The watermelon man certainly returns to a trailer or a house. At the end of the day the sign-maker hoists himself with difficulty up the school bus steps while the woman folds his wheelchair at the bottom. The wind-screw man might live anywhere.

Or maybe when they leave the corner they simply disappear like old election signs and windborne trash. But no: once on a wet day you meet the walker dressed in a slicker and realize that somewhere on his route he must have some kind of home. He is always clean-shaven.

The trees vanish on December 26, just as the pumpkins did on November 1. The regular vendors work through the holidays, and after New Year's the sign-maker produces a larger one than usual:

THE GODS DO NOT DEDUCT
FROM MAN'S ALLOTTED SPAN
THE HOURS SPENT IN FISHING

Now the watermelon man turns to citrus. He brings out a few crates of oranges, and he advertises:

ARIZONA SWEETS

Then he adds grapefruit and a second sign:

FREE SAMPLES

Munching one himself, he swings his legs from the tailgate in the winter sunshine. A single waist-high windmill rotates on the ground near his truck. The dog hopes for a handout. The wind screw man chats with the sign bus woman. The child sits beside the sign-maker. None of the vendors come when it rains.

But rain is rare, and soon there are symptoms of spring. The walker sports a new baseball cap. And then, just before Valentine's Day, the corner is invaded by teenaged girls selling flowers. They hawk their bouquets in the edge of the traffic, so it's easy to see that both the flowers and the girls have lost their original freshness. The blonde woman lounges beneath the wind-screw man's awning, and she holds a bunch of flowers on her lap. Above her head the screws spin furiously in the wind.

One day when you reach the drop-off there is a magical garden down below. Fresh green leaves have popped up overnight: ficus trees and aloes and rhododendron bushes, potted palms, mystery shrubs with red and blue blossoms, and cherry trees in full bloom.

The silk plants don't last long. They are followed by a truck full of lawn furniture laid out on a stripe of Astroturf, and then by a seller of pseudo-Navajo and pseudo-Persian rugs. The rugs are replaced by a crowd of painted statuettes: tigers, ducks, heads of lions, clowns, screaming eagles, gnomes, Santas, naked ladies, coiled rattlesnakes, black and white jockeys, Jack and Bobby Kennedys, sleeping Mexicans, tramps, Spanish dancers, and Bambis. Another day, inflatable Easter bunnies as big as Dobermans flap from a string. Once for some unknown reason a moving van spends the night parked on the vacant lot at the corner. A single enormous red word leaps from the side of the van:

SECURITY

Often during this period you meet the walker at the top of the hill. Stern and strong, he now carries a long staff in his hand like some archaic figure, and he fixes his eyes straight ahead.

Summer begins early in May, with watermelons in abundance. It has not rained for two months, and from the top of the big hill the city looks like the dregs of a lumpy liquid. The heat sets in. The bedraggled flower girls return for a Mother's Day so witheringly hot that by afternoon they have hidden themselves and their unsold bouquets in the shadow thrown by the watermelon man's truck. The wind-screw man seems to be gone (has he migrated north with the tourists?) The sign bus remains, and the sign-maker's silhouette is visible inside. He has posted something new:

GRAVITY IS WINNING

When you reach the drop-off a few days later, you come upon the scene of a disaster. Police are directing traffic around a tangle of smoking junk in the middle of the intersection. A few firefighters hose it while others scatter sawdust in the dark pools that remain on the asphalt, and others whisk broken glass to the edge of the pavement with push brooms. A lone shoe lies abandoned in the street, and little clumps of onlookers stand in silence as an ambulance pulls slowly away.

On a warm velvety night not long after this, the corner is radiant, lit up like a carnival. There are phosphorescent doodles upon the darkness: a pink flamingo, a turquoise cactus, a golden coyote, and an emerald palm tree. Someone is peddling neon sculptures. (But can that really be a neon heart oozing neon blood drip-drip-drip?)

The next time you pass in the daylight you find the bus and the truck, the sign-maker, the watermelon man, and the dog. Where are the woman and the child? Once, later, at a distance in another part of town, you think you catch a glimpse of the wind-screw man, but you are not sure. Day after day the sign bus parks at the same corner, until finally you see the white-haired child again, but never again the woman.

The walker frowns, for the first time betraying emotion: uncertainty, even fear. Instead of striding purposefully forward, he wobbles, he labors. His progress is painfully slow. He is riding a bicycle.

The last wooden sign is very long and thin. The black lettering almost spills off the wood:

O WORLD, O LIFE, O TIME

Afterward, the old man alone continues to offer watermelons, striped as well as solid green, and cantaloupes the size and weight of a baby's head. After a month or two, he spray-paints a new message on a sheet of cardboard:

SEEDLESS
SUPERB

The walker abandons his bicycle and becomes a walker again.

Then one morning the corner is empty. A primitive fence surrounds the little spot of scraped earth, and from a single strand of wire dangle half a dozen signs, all reading:

PRIVATE PROPERTY
KEEP OUT

The plants creep in. Nothing can stop the desert broom or the shapely pigweed. And there's a fine silver-green crop of Russian thistles springing up: before you know it, they'll be tumbleweeds.

Ironwork

Inexorable as a stopwatch, a tiny yellow airplane crept across the clear blue sky. And then Rascoe watched it pop like a grain of corn.

He lay flat on his back, looking up. Birthday candles flickered all around him quite innocently until one little flame began to scorch his left arm, and then, smelling burnt hair, or maybe flesh, he gave a full-body jerk and found himself wide awake and sweaty. His heart punched unmercifully at his breastbone.

"Hell and death!"

Rascoe swung his legs, which looked oddly younger than the rest of him, over the edge of the bed and decided to get up, pitch-black as the world still was.

"Dream like that—clear sign this night is over. Nothing else!" he said aloud, combatively. "Interpretation of dreams! Damn stupid stuff! Yah!"

He wasn't afraid of fire, either, for he knew fire, worked with it daily in his metal shop. In fact, fire figured in one of his earliest memories. Someone must have caught him playing with matches but he had forgotten that part. The memory began when his father seized Rascoe's hand in his special safety grip (one big finger hooked through Rascoe's small ones, the other four handcuffed around Rascoe's skinny wrist) and led him toward a heap of dry leaves. "Now watch!" His father dropped a burning match, and they leaped backward hand in hand and watched as flames lapped up the leaves until they hit the hidden firecracker and blew it sky high. This was supposed to teach him to fear fire, but Rascoe loved everything about it. He loved it still.

Yesterday's clothes would do. They usually did, often for weeks on end. He placed a heavy silver bracelet on his left wrist and his sweat-stiff baseball cap on his head and made a proclamation.

"I don't care if you're God or some Viennese quack or Señora Luna the damn palm reader, you're a charlatan and a bloodsucker and I don't want you spooking around inside my head!"

Rascoe operated according to rules—many, many of them. He believed in truth, logic, and reason, but he also believed that the world was a dangerous place because its natural patterns were constantly twisted by humans. The great machine would function perfectly, he thought, if billions of evil monkeys didn't mess with it.

"Chimps with car keys!" Rascoe muttered, searching for his own.

There were certain defenses: Rascoe was a measurer and a counter. Stair steps and hammer blows must always be carefully numbered, and daily routines must be followed, and any disruption to patterns must be vigorously counterattacked if possible. There were certain glints in the darkness, though—a few rare flashes of grace. Also there were certain unaccountable phenomena that he wanted to disbelieve but could not quite. They laid eggs under his skin.

Still muttering, he revved up the bulbous old pickup that he'd nicknamed The Elephant's Child and headed out into the warm black gases of the night. The other car in his driveway, a 1931 Packard, hadn't moved in decades. Bermuda grass was beginning to penetrate its four flat white-wall tires, and beneath its hood, generations of pack rats had built a stinking ziggurat of cactus segments, excrement, and stolen property from Rascoe's house, including a Pueblo fetish carved from a deer antler, several anchovy cans, a tangled chain, the back door key, and one fresh rose apparently transformed by legerdemain into a rust-red blossom of iron.

"Some people hate nightmares," Rascoe said, turning left

fast, tires squealing, eyes gleaming. "I eat 'em up. I rate 'em like movies." He stopped at the seedy 7-Eleven store that served the neighborhood near his home-slash-shop, bought his usual pint of black coffee—last night's boiled-down engine oil at this ungodly hour—and, as was his habit, paused by the stack of virgin newspapers to read the headlines in the *Arizona Daily Star* for July 17, 1999.

CLINTON WINS BUDGET; MORE LIES AHEAD

"Politicians," observed Rascoe with satisfaction. He liked to see his dark theories borne out. "You'd think they'd get tired of themselves after a while, but no-o-o."

The recent presidential impeachment scandal had been meat and drink to him for months on end, and he missed it sadly. Still, this was some consolation. He added the headline to his private collection of rampant human nonsense, filed away in the jiggly globs of his brain somewhere between "hatred" and "humor," and gave it two stars. Rascoe never allowed himself to open a newspaper without paying for it, but his personal code did permit a quick glance at the bottom half of the front page. So he turned the paper over and the headline jumped at him:

JFK JR. LOST IN PLANE CRASH

"No," he said, spilling coffee. Deep in his intestines he felt a Southern Baptist quiver. "Small planes are never yellow," he thought. "It couldn't be. No!"

A few days later another headline leaped at him and caused an expectoration of coffee on the floor:

SOMETHING WENT WRONG IN PLANE CRASH, EXPERTS SAY

Three stars. Nineteen ninety-nine must be a good year for

idiocy, he thought, but what year wasn't? Millennium? End times? Apocalypse? Bah! He squelched *those* ridiculous ideas, and off he went to his work.

The fire in the forge lit up his shop just enough to work by. Rascoe thrust an iron rod into the heart of the forge and watched the color change from gray to dark red, suitable for surface finishing. Bright red meant the iron was malleable, yellow indicated the correct temperature for forging, and white for welding. The coincidence of dream and headline was odd, Rascoe thought, but odd was normal. When the iron turned yellow, he laid it on the anvil and hammered it flat with nineteen short fierce strokes. He was constructing a latch for the garden gate of a man who had made a fortune by plowing down thousands of acres of desert trees and cactus and cramming shoddy houses there instead.

He'd asked Rascoe for something Western, something special, and Rascoe thought it over and said, "Carte blanche, eh?" The developer gave a thumbs-up, so Rascoe designed the apparatus in the shape of a jackass. The latch itself was the off hind leg, complete with miniature shoe, which kicked.

The customer seemed delighted with his iron ass and made a special phone call to thank Rascoe personally.

"Quirky, aren't you?" he said.

"Quirky!"

Rascoe slammed down first the phone, then the visor of his welding helmet. "Quirky!" He ejaculated the word inside the helmet, smearing the screen. "Ha! Faugh! Quirk *you!*"

"You . . . walking Porta-Potty! You . . . cancerous chupaca-bras!" He hissed and spat out his consonants.

Then: "*Vegan!*"

The welding machine sizzled, disgorging a swarm of stars too bright for a naked eye to bear.

Summer flowed toward fall. Then one night a bouquet

bloomed from the top of a distant cone in sprays of red, orange, yellow, and white fire. Gray objects began to fall around Rascoe, crashing down higgledy-piggledy, sprawled figures, life-size, face down. "Dummies?" thought Rascoe. "No," answered one of them, raising himself on his elbows. "Plaster casts." Rascoe tried to yell and nothing came out but a suffocated grunt.

"Okay. Fine. Olé! Touché!" he taunted the universe. "Two and a half stars—*maybe* three."

It was the first dream of the night. He'd fallen asleep on his slump of a couch with the lights on, reading. Now the book lay spatchcocked like a grilled chicken on the floor while his collection of Hopi kachinas and New Mexican santos looked down calmly from the wall. Rascoe stood up, barefoot on grit. In the yard outside his front door, which summer or winter he rarely shut, a small sand dune took shape, then trickled over the threshold and progressed across the room.

"You don't know and you don't care," Rascoe told the kachinas and santos. This was a comforting thought. What good companions they were, so blessedly mute. That was one reason why he liked them.

He extinguished the light, went to his bed, and forgot all about it until the next morning when he passed the stack of newspapers at the 7-Eleven. The day's date was, he noted carefully, September 4, 1999. He couldn't help reading the banner headline below the date, and it did not disappoint.

WAR DIMS HOPES FOR PEACE

"Ha!" said Rascoe in a voice like a rasp on rusty iron and he stopped for a moment or two just to savor the words. That line might even rate ten stars, he thought. Inadvertent truth—boy howdy, what a world it was! Sometimes he really longed for an errant asteroid to smite it all to smithereens (but perhaps not till he finished his current work, which was going well). Next he turned the paper over and came upon another headline:

MASSIVE ERUPTION ON MT. ETNA

He examined a picture of a Sicilian religious procession holding up a cross to stop the lava. *Lava*, he thought. Then he drove his coffee home, steering carefully while not thinking about Pompeii.

"Nothing to do with me." He took up his tools. The blunt sad features of the plaster man kept bobbing to the surface of his mind, hinting otherwise, but this time Rascoe clamped down and willed his innards not to quiver.

The work of the day was burglar bars for the home of a woman who was well known, locally at least, for her paintings of scenes of violence on canvases that she sometimes deliberately slashed and burned. She lived alone in a remote house where every detail was so exquisite that even the dog's bones were arranged in a formal pattern beside its dish, but she had taken to dropping too frequently by Rascoe's shop to see how the bars were progressing.

"And here she comes again," he mumbled through his teeth as he twisted an iron rod like a piece of taffy. "Dripping *fringe*, for God's sake."

"Rascoe," she said, "I wish you'd do something more for me."

"Like what?"

"Well . . ." She came a little too close to his fire. "I love the way you make iron do things it really can't do, how you mold it like clay, and I want you to make me one of your little sculptures. I don't care what it is. You decide."

"Watch out," he said, waving the dull red rod, and she took a step backward. Over the years his hands had hardened, so he could touch things that would blister thinner skins. Rascoe selected a chisel for the next step. "There are some pitiful shysters," he said, "and I hope to hell I'm not one of 'em, who pretend a '*blacksmith*' has some damn mystical vocation, that he's an '*artist*' instead of a plain iron worker, a smutty-handed common craftsman, John Smith, period, the end. Yah! Do you really make paint do things it can't do?"

A few weeks later, a black widow spider would hang in a web of delicate iron threads, almost but not quite concealing the doorbell of the painter's isolated house. She ceased to visit Rascoe's workshop, and to his surprise he felt a prickle of regret. He was of two minds about her. Nothing ever tasted as delicious to him as righteous rage, and yet—and yet—could it be that he almost missed being annoyed by her?

Once, for another woman, he had made an iron door covered with hummingbirds and flowers, but that was very long ago in Taos, and she was dead. Every so often The Elephant's Child would be seen parked outside a bar, which, according to the very few people who knew him, meant that the mood had seized Rascoe to pick up a man, just any old one-night man, inside.

In early October he received a commission from a historic church to complete its unfinished ironwork, so he built a magnificent structure of spirals and tendrils into which he inserted tiny befuddled sheep. For another client he forged a fence topped with spikes and secured with cunning locks— "I.Q.-test locks," he called them—all nearly impenetrable by the average Joe including the client, and each completely made by hand.

Sometimes he turned work down. When a woman requested a doorknocker in the shape of a hand, he demanded more information. Whose door? Why a hand? It was to be a gift, she said, and as he listened he felt the eggs itch under his skin. Something was not right.

"You can't go imposing a gift on someone," he scolded. "*It* has a say in the matter too. Does she really want it? Probably not. Go find a *blacksmith*, lady."

And she went.

On the day before Halloween, along with his morning coffee Rascoe collected a new headline that clearly was not connected to his dreams, which now sloshed around his head as dull as old gray laundry in a tub. In fact, the nightmare factory seemed to have gone out of business. The headline read:

MINERS REFUSE TO WORK AFTER DEATH

The idea of a ghost strike delighted Rascoe (who throughout his whole career had never worked successfully in any group) so much that he kept breaking out in smiles at odd moments all day long. "Yah! Twenty-seven stars!" he chortled. In the middle of Halloween night, however, he started up abruptly: huge, thick, glossy, fake crimson poppies filled his field of vision.

Well, now, so what? This dream was based on *The Wizard of Oz*, no doubt about it. He lay down again and remembered the first time he'd seen the movie in 1954, when he was eleven years old and a kid in Texas. He saw it seven times in two days. And then he went home and made models of every character in the movie, including a wicked witch who flew circles on the end of a wire.

"Dun-da-dun-da-DA-da! Dun-da-dun-da-DA-da! DA! DA!" He hummed the witch's theme in the dark.

It was almost time to visit his parents again. Every few years he went back to Dallas, back to the decaying house with the perpetual leak in the front lawn and the smell of butane gas in the kitchen and methane in the bathroom, crossing Texas on the train, two days over and two days back. He had his reasons. For one, The Elephant's Child was known to play tricks on long trips, and Rascoe dreaded being marooned someplace like the west Texas town that he always called "Odesolate." And of course the days he spent on the train were days he did not have to spend at home.

Yes. Yes. This might be the last time, Rascoe thought, and hallelujah. But what would become of his sister when their parents were gone? Surely his loudmouth aunt and cousins would snatch her away, as well as anything else of possible value. Nobody expected *him* to take a hand. No, he'd gone straight from home to hell, even if he did come back sometimes to visit. And even though home and hell were not much different, that gang of females wouldn't let his sister's six-year-old mentality come anywhere near an outlaw like him. He would miss their gentle little conversations, though, for his sister's mind was completely straightforward. Once again he mentally replayed his last exchange with his aunt.

Rascoe (screaming): "Just give me an honest answer!"

Aunt: (screaming louder): "Well, you'll never get *that* from me!"

So the nightmare factory was definitely closed. And anyway, weird dreams had nothing to do with the other events of the world or his life, including the work he did, the quarrels he picked, or the amount of marijuana he smoked. No way. He checked his guts for quivers and found none. "I'm over it," he told himself jubilantly.

These were his thoughts the next morning as he battered a lump of metal into the shape of a chipmunk with bulging eyes and cheeks, which was intended to perch on a post outside an art gallery in Santa Fe. He stared the chubby chipmunk straight in the eye. "Never do anything you're not paid for. Twenty dollars an hour plus expenses. Materials in cash, labor by check. The hell with the critics—what do your creditors say? Yah! Ironwork is what it is, and that's the truth."

It was some days later that Rascoe first heard about the Egyptian pilot who flew his jet into the Atlantic on Halloween, chanting "Allahu Akbar!" all the way down. Rascoe had actually overlooked those headlines because he was distracted by two others:

MAN STRUCK BY LIGHTNING FACES
BATTERY CHARGE

and

KIDS MAKE NUTRITIOUS SNACKS

These made Rascoe laugh till he almost bought the paper, and somehow the Egyptian airplane disaster struck him as equally preposterous, if unfunny. He was over it, wasn't he? So he pushed it all away and went back to work.

But on the night of November 17, 1999, he had another dream. Dressed in his old Aggie uniform, he was dragging a telephone pole toward a great intricate tower of other combustible material. When he got there, he pulled off his arms one after the other and tossed them onto the pyre, for now it had begun to burn.

"God's death!" Rascoe discovered that he was sitting on the edge of his bed. Dawn was breaking outside, a frosty desert dawn, and although his arms were now reattached, he was furious. "No visions! No prophesies! No damn UFO's! No aliens! No angels! Scram! Git!"

That morning's *Star* reported that a thousand miles away in College Station the great annual Texas A & M bonfire, usually a marvel of engineering, had collapsed and killed twelve people. Rascoe sat very still in The Elephant's Child outside the 7-Eleven and counted his breaths for a long time before he could start the engine. Years ago he had helped to build those Aggie bonfires. Must be a rational explanation. He couldn't possibly have known. No. No. No. But the inner quivers came back, now raised to a higher power. He canceled his Thanksgiving trip to Texas.

And as the days grew shorter and the year inched toward its end, he noticed more and more warnings, both in the news that he couldn't avoid and in bits of bonehead gabble that he happened to overhear.

THE END IS NEAR

COMPUTER DISASTER

Y2K Y2K Y2K Y2K

"Devil's snare!" hissed Rascoe, who rejected computers and all their works. Somewhere beneath a layer of greasy dust he did possess a radio, but he utterly scorned television. "Pathetic wiggling guff," he called it. And now he did not want to know too much, particularly if some kind of doomsday was on the way. Surely it was not. But what if—? He felt yet another quiver move out of his small intestine and wrap around his back, where it turned into ripple after ripple of chills. From memories of sermons, he dimly recalled signs of the end of the world. Not that any of them seemed to be happening.

"Trees bleed," he said out loud. "Stones fight each other . . ." Rascoe washed his hands in the water he used to cool his iron and temper his steel. "Dead bones rise from their graves, constellations fall from the sky," he murmured, rubbing leftover dirt from his hands onto his shorts. "And it's the end! Yah! No more anything, no more knaves and idiots, no more lies!" he gloated. "Good riddance!"

But of course it wasn't. At least, not yet.

Late one afternoon in the middle of December, he turned

from what he was doing and saw a figure outlined in the open doorway. To his surprise he recognized his former customer, the black widow. Although the breeze was cold, she was dressed in pale filmy clothes, and in one hand she carried a package like a silver brick.

"You again," said Rascoe, feeling a slight, not unpleasant, fizz.

"Congratulations!" she said. "I heard you won an award."

He snorted. "Awards!" he said. "They fall from the sky like pigeon poop."

"But is it better *not* to get them?"

"Paugh," said Rascoe, shrugging.

"So, what are you up to now?"

"Barbecuing," he said. He stood aside to reveal a thickly crusted grill with something smoking on top.

She laughed in a friendly way but made no move to enter. "You cook in your workshop?"

"Why not?"

"Actually, I meant to ask what you're making now. In metal."

Rascoe waved an arm toward a distant table where a large toad appeared to be squatting in the gloom.

"May I?" she asked. Gathering her veils and draperies close, she came forward and gingerly touched the amphibian.

"Oh! I really thought it was alive! Or maybe . . . dead. What's this over here?"

"Fire screen," he answered in a gruff voice. He jerked his chin toward her other hand. "What's *that*?"

"I brought you a present," she said.

"Ha!"

"Made it myself. Just wondered how you were."

"I'm working." She said nothing. Then he blurted it out: "Not sleeping."

She studied him closely. "I'm sorry. The work is good."

"I dream dreams."

"Nightmares?"

"Airplane crashes," he said. "Among other things."

"You don't fly, do you?"

Rascoe lost control. "*Do you see wings?*" he shrieked.

"Don't you *ever* take your armor off?" yelled the widow, retreating a step.

"I *prefer* trains," he said loudly.

"God! They'll never cremate you, Rascoe! They'll have to melt you down!" She turned to examine the fire screen. "Oh, maybe I put my foot in my mouth. Again."

When the wrought iron doors of the screen stood open, the human eye perceived nothing but angles and arcs, but when the widow clanged the two sides together, a design snapped out. "Of course, a monster. Perfect!"

"No, it's not."

"Then what is it?"

"Not a monster. It's a goddamn phoenix and goddamn imperfect."

"Oh yes, me too, but I keep on dabbing." She spoke gently: "Mustn't let the great be the enemy of the not bad at all."

"Are you still slashing and burning?" Rascoe asked.

"No," she said. "I'm done with it. I'm in a new phase." She pursed her lips, then added: "Those paintings didn't exactly fly out of the gallery, you know."

"This is my last," said Rascoe, turning his eyes from the phoenix to the filthy floor. "I'm running out of time."

"How can you say that? Who's it for?"

"Nobody. Me." Now the words came rattling like handfuls of gravel: "I dreamed a head of gold, chest and arms of silver, belly of brass, legs of iron, feet of clay . . ."

"Whoa!"

"Tried to weld 'em on and they wouldn't stick. End times. Dreams. In some cockamamie way they keep coming true even though I don't believe in them and they're driving me crazy." He whacked his workbench hard with his greasy spatula.

She pondered.

"Are you talking about the millennium?"

Smoke puffed upward from the grill behind him, followed by the smell of burning flesh. He felt the shop floor tip and spin as though he and she were riding a cosmic Tilt-a-Whirl together. Every iron atom in his blood began to scream.

"Even dreams are dreams," the widow said, dreamily shaking her head.

"Stop it! Stop it right now!"

"What I believe in," she went on, ignoring his yells, "though you didn't ask, is the long hairy arm of coincidence. Oh, there'll be plenty of disasters, never fear, but if there is such a thing as the millennium, which I doubt, it's sure as hell not two weeks from now."

"What?"

"Next year *can't* really be the year two thousand because there never was a year zero. Do the arithmetic."

As he stared at her, his workshop steadied and brightened, and with each breath—four, five, six, ten—he seemed to suck a little more oxygen. Ah yes, he thought, yes, yes, pure sweet math. His skin stopped itching and the chaos inside his head settled into a tolerable shape.

"We have at least another year," she added casually and clutched at her veils as they wandered away on a gust of cold air.

Rascoe recognized a moment of grace when it walloped him between the eyeballs. He checked the grill. The chicken was burnt on the outside and probably raw inside, but somewhere between the skin and the bone he thought there must be something good to eat.

"Stay for dinner?" he asked.

With infinitely slow and cautious movements the widow crept close to him. Then she held out her package.

"Fruitcake," she said.

LOVE AND DEATH

Eight Short
Short Stories

I. Wheat Country Weddings

1.

Bride's pregnant,
maid of honor, too . . .
both by the groom.
Groom and maid vanish from the reception,
but return
from the dead.

2.

1960: The bride is pregnant, as is her maid of honor. (Same father: the groom.)
Groom and maid flee the reception together.
1967: They're declared legally dead.
1992: A strange RV arrives at the groom's old home. A family spills out.
Oddly, it seems they've never been gone.

3.

First comes the wheat harvest, then the wedding. Everybody knows everybody in this little town, so everybody's invited. The bride and groom are high-school sweethearts; their parents' farms lie side by side. This is Kansas, the year is 1960, and the bride is all white lace from head to neck to wrist to toe. She's pregnant, but everything is going to be fine. Afterward, she smiles down the aisle, followed by the maid of honor, all pink taffeta from collarbone to knee. And the maid of honor's pregnant too. Both by the groom.

The reception begins and the marriage ends.

4.

Wheat harvest runs through June, so the wedding is set for

July. And there's a bumper crop in 1960, fifty bushels an acre, so the groom and best man follow the harvest from Kansas to Oklahoma, Nebraska, and South Dakota almost into Canada, running combines. They come home with their pockets full of stubble and money, just in time for the ceremony.

The church is packed. In such a small farm town everybody knows everything about everybody—or almost—and they all want to witness this long-expected event. The bride and groom have been going steady since eighth grade; their families' farms border on each other. It's a typical wedding: first bridesmaids, then maid of honor, all rose-colored ruffles and puff sleeves. Except for her head and hands, the bride is completely dressed in white. She smiles both up and down the aisle, but the groom and maid of honor can't quite. What the three of them know, and nobody else, is that the bride is pregnant, and so is the maid of honor, and the father of both babies is the groom.

In the middle of the reception, as the bride dances with the best man, the groom approaches the maid of honor, sets his trembling right hand on her taffeta waist and asks her to run away with him. It proves fairly easy to disappear, and they do. The three families hear absolutely nothing, so seven years later the bride has the groom declared legally dead and remarries.

Wheat harvest follows wheat harvest. Funerals follow weddings follow christenings. Not a word. And then one day a recreational vehicle pulls up at the old farmhouse where the groom used to live, and his shocked elderly parents watch a family emerge from it. Choose one (or more):

A. They're the undead.

B. The runaways fled to wheat-farming country in Canada where they thrived, and now, after the great harvest of 1992, they've finally come home.

C. Pure dementia!

II. Black Decal

In the Rear Window of a Dented Gray 1992 Toyota Corolla

In loving memory of Nadia Maria Carbajal

April 12, 1987–February 27, 2011

WATCH OUT FOR MOTORCYCLES

III. M + N

Dearest M,

I bought a house. Oh, it's the most wonderful house! It has a turquoise door with a tiny brass hand for a knocker, and a secret room (well, maybe just a cupboard, but I can fit inside), and I know it's the next right step for me. I do have to keep repeating that phrase to myself. It's daunting to be responsible for everything all by myself.

Once the house belonged to a feisty little widow. After she died, it sat vacant for almost two years until her son decided to sell it. Why did he wait so long? I don't know, or maybe I do know, because two years was just the right time for me, too.

Unpacking all my boxes has been very emotional. In everything I open, there you are—boxes of nails labeled in your handwriting, your tools, your guns—as well as all of our shared things. It's quiet here. From my bedroom window I can see the sky. At night I watch the moon set, and the Pleiades. And then till sunrise I lie alone.

I'm trying hard to be strong. It helps to think of this house going from one feisty little widow to another. But oh, I love you so much, and I miss you more than words can say. I would go into the wooden embrace of my secret room and come straight to you if only I knew where you are.

I *am* certain that this will reach you, and we will meet again, and for that I am grateful.

Love always, always,

N

IV. Getting Hitched

It was one hell of a wedding. The bride's cowboy brothers came after the groom with their castration knives, and the priest jumped in and tackled them, and while he had one of these guys pinned down he gasped out to the mother of the bride, trying to reassure her (she always drove around in a pink Cadillac, which was actually the cause of the quarrel): "Don't worry! This happens all the time!"

V. The Carpathian Mountains

☎ ☎ ☎ ☎

"Hello?"

"Al?"

"Who's calling?"

"Alexander Lemko?"

"Ha! You called before. Wrong number. Goodbye."

☎ ☎ ☎ ☎

"Hello?"

"You *are* Alexander Lemko, aren't you? It's not a common name."

"Well, there are at least two of us, because I am not your man. I told you so before. Please. Stop. Calling."

"Alexander Joseph Lemko? Age 60? On Fairview Drive?"

"Obviously you looked me up. However, I am not the Lemko who skipped out on his phone bill."

"But—"

"Nor am I the Lemko who failed to return his wretched rental Jeep in Omaha."

"How—"

"And I am definitely not the Alexander Lemko whose ex-wife Rhonda is gunning for him."

"I—"

"You've got the wrong number. Please don't call again."

"But how—"

"Go look somewhere else. You're beating a dead horse."

"What?"

"It's called a figure of speech. Look, by nature and training I'm a cultured, courteous, patient fellow. That's why we're still talking. But now it's time to say goodbye."

"Wait! If you aren't him, how'd you know those things?"

"Others have called me, too, of course, dozens of them seemingly in search of this Lemko chap. But when I explained that I was not he, they stopped."

"Could he be a relative?"

"No. Goodbye."

☎ ☎ ☎ ☎

"Hello? Sorry, Al, just one more thing. What if he's stolen your identity?"

"My accounts are all in order. I am not Al. No one has ever called me Al in all my life except for you. Now, let me ask *you* a few questions for a change. You seem young—are you?"

"I—"

"Do they pay you enough for this? Is there a nice fat bounty on the head of the elusive Lemko?"

"No, sir. Not really."

"You've got a bad job. You should quit."

"Quit!"

"There are lots of better jobs. Go find one."

"Why?"

"Very well then, listen carefully. My people are from the Carpathian Mountains. Do you know where that is?"

"No."

"You can look it up."

"What?"

"And if you don't stop calling me, I'll put a curse on you."

"What?"

"I'll put a curse on you."

"Hey!"

"You heard me. Goodbye."

☎ ☎ ☎ ☎

"You can't do that!"

"Oh yes I can. Let me tell you a story. Do you have a moment? Oh wait! Of course you do. Well, once upon a time I lived next door to a very annoying woman. I suffered through barking dogs, littering, property-line encroachment, music—*bad* music—way past midnight, and so, eventually, having exhausted all other civilized options without success, I called her up and told her that my people were from the Carpathian Mountains."

"You did?"

"And she said, 'What are you talking about?' So I said, 'You can look it up. And by the way, I'm putting a curse on you.' Just like you, she said, 'You can't do that!' And so I told her, 'Just you wait.'"

"What happened?"

"Let's just say she's not my neighbor anymore."

"What do you mean?"

"Goodbye for good and don't call back."

☎ ☎ ☎ ☎

"Son, you really need to improve your listening skills. Didn't you understand the story? *Don't call me.*"

"But—"

"AAAAAAAAAAAAhhhhhh!"

"Listen, Mr. Lemko, if you think you can threaten me—"

"I'm not threatening anybody. I'm simply stating the truth."

"I never heard of any Carpathian Mountains."

"Have you ever heard of Vlad the Impaler?"

"What's that?"

"Think shish kebob, my friend. Human shish kebob."

"But—"

"Listen. My daughter is an aspiring actress. So a few years ago she moved to New York. That's the best place for actors to aspire, you know."

"Why are you telling me this?"

"She needed to find an affordable place to live, which was harder to do than either aspiring or acting. But at last she called in ecstasies of joy. She'd found the most marvelous apartment! And the rent was incredibly low! The landlady was Austrian, such a lovely lady! So my daughter gave her a check for two thousand dollars right on the spot. 'And I'm moving in tomorrow!' she told me."

"You're just trying to throw me off the track."

"No, son. My intentions are good. In spite of how obnoxious you are, I really do feel sorry for you. So pay attention. My daughter called me back an hour later. 'Dad, Dad, I've made a terrible mistake. It's not a dream apartment after all. She's the worst landlady in New York! There's a whole website about her, horrible stories posted by angry tenants. What shall I do?' So I told my daughter to go and demand her check back immediately."

"No landlady would do that in a million years!"

"That's what my daughter said. But she went back anyway, after I'd asked for the landlady's phone number and advised my daughter to take an umbrella with her."

"What?"

"When she arrived, my daughter set her phone on 'speaker.' So I heard everything, first her knocking, and then I heard her ask politely for her check back. But the woman just laughed and refused to open the door."

"So?"

"I told my daughter to bang on the door with the umbrella and keep asking again and again, and meanwhile I called the landlady's phone again and again. No answer, but her neighbors heard all the ruckus and began to creep out into the hall to watch."

"And?"

"'My people are from the Carpathian Mountains,' cried out my daughter. I heard the landlady give a gasp. Of course Austria's not far from the Carpathian Mountains. You probably didn't know that either, did you?"

"No."

"Well, now you do. 'And I'll put a curse on you!' my daughter vowed, in a splendid voice that inspired me with great hope for her future career because instantly the door cracked open. Out flew the check! And then all the spectators broke into applause."

"I don't get it."

"Think harder."

"But——"

"Good——bye."

☎ ☎ ☎ ☎

"I *told* you not to call me. Haven't you ever heard of werewolves? Vampires? You must have heard of Dracula?"

"You have to be kidding!"

"No, my friend, I very rarely kid."

"Don't try to scare me with some dumb hokey threat——"

"I warned you about the curse. Sorry! Here goes! You'll crash your car. You'll knock out your front teeth. Your mother will be arrested . . . for soliciting. And aren't you starting to itch? Your girlfriend will leave you. You'll be trolled on the internet. Your potted plants will shrivel completely up, along with your penis, and you'll never, ever stop talking like Donald Duck. Did I mention chronic diarrhea? It should be starting by now. Can't you tell? How do you feel? Is it working? Are you itching yet?"

"You can't do that!"

"Oh yes I can!"

☎ ☎ ☎

"Wait! Wait! Don't hang up! Talk to me! It's not real, is it? Is it?"

☎ ☎ ☎ ☎
☎ ☎ ☎ ☎

"Who are you? Why me? Oh God! I feel sick. I *am* itching. Stop it! Stop it right now! You *are* him, aren't you? I knew it, I knew it! Alexander Joseph Lemko, answer me!"

☎ ☎ ☎ ☎
☎ ☎ ☎ ☎
☎ ☎ ☎ ☎

☎ ☎ ☎ ☎
☎ ☎ ☎ ☎

☎

VI. Bumper Sticker

On a Hunter's Truck Parked by the Side of the Road

J. B. TAXIDERMY

LONGER THAN LIFE

VII. Cereus Monstrous

Gotta weapon? Gotta use it!

Got two? Load 'em up and go go go. Gun control? HEH! Use two hands! Go where? Outta here, somewhere, anywhere far from her. Go gettum! Get that rifle sighted in. Out in the desert. But beer. Forgot beer. Forget her. Go get beer.

Get outta Dodge. Nowhere! Forget. Forget it. Stop it. Beer up, drive on, way out into the dirty desert, ass end of the godforsaken world. Butt-ugly. Freedom is green. Fences are aggression. Enemies. Pricks. Monsters. Your life is not my fault. Her life is not my fault. Everything is her fault.

Rifle. To sight it in, bullet holes in paper. Point of impact = POI. Dead eye. Bull's eye. Where's that target? Ahhh, there it is, beneath the beer. Now where the hell's the other one? The human one?

.	.	.	.	.	.
sun	air	water	dirt	sky	time
.	.	.	.	.	.

O.K. Set the target 25 yards away. Then 50. Then 100. Measure how? Guess. Check accuracy each distance. Goddamn stickers everywhere. Goddamn cactus. Green skin. Arms. Pillars, soldiers, aliens, monsters. And everything stings, bites, strikes needles. Just waiting to jump me. Don't tread on me.

Settle down now, really concentrate, squeeze the trigger. Go deaf.

Killology they call it. Study killing. Fire groups of shots. Deaf. Damn! All of 'em missed the bull's eye, high and wide to the right. Measure?

Goddamn stupid math. "Calculate relation between cross-hairs and POI"? No, can't do it. Won't do it. Be a man, just spin the dial and eye it in! Bam bam bam. Deaf. Missed.

.   .   .   .

Larrea   *Opuntia Cereus*   *Cercidium*   *Fouquieria*

Greasewood Prickly Pear Giant Cactus Palo Verde Tree Ocotillo

.   .   .   .

Try again. Different target. Wussy shooting ranges ban human targets! Body to waist. Circles around the heart. Sex? What sex? Not sure. Say it's her. What she did to me! Forget it. Hi ho the bitch is dead, bitch cop, bitch judge, bitch doctor, bitch Hillary, bitch Nancy, all of 'em make me sick. Sluts, skanks, whores. Ditch the bitch. Lock her up.

Forget it. Settle down now, focus. Breathe. Go for the heart.

Bam bam bam bam. Deaf. Missed.

.   .   .   .

arms   ribs   spines   heads   trunks

.   .   .   .

Big green aliens, mutants everywhere. Butt-ugly. My rights don't end where your feelings begin. The hell with feelings and the hell with you and the hell with sighting it in, just shoot another target. What else have I got? Bud Light, tepid water. Throw it away, get a cold one.

Beer can?

Bam bam BAM. Finally!

Beer can blew up. Lock her up. Need another target. Need another beer. Feel around under the seat . . . greasy wrappers . . . shotgun shells . . . *Playboy*! Perfect. Stick it on a tree branch, stand back. Suck it up, buttercup.

.   .   .   .

stand   still   survive

.   .   .   .

Shoot 'em up. Shoot 'em in the pussy. Shoot 'em in the butt, boobs, mouth, head, eyes, hair. Your life is not my fault. My life is not your business. *Playboy* holes, nothing but holes. Deaf deaf deaf deaf. Good. Good aim up close. Shoot more. All fall down. What now? Reload. Beer.

.   .   .   .

I   I   I   I
        I

                                I I   I

I   I I

.   .   .   .

These goddamn cactus things are getting on my nerves. Pussies in green pantsuits. Ganging up on me, standing around. Waiting. Monsters. Monsters. Missed! Get up close.

Crest

Hole

Rib

Arm Arm

    Arm Arm Arm

Rib

  Spine

Rib

Trunk

  Dirt

Roots

.   .   .   .

Missed. Missed again. Use both hands. Focus. Goddamn wobble.

Hey, genius! Try the shotgun? Double barrel, spray shot. Close range. *Get* those boogers. Load. Beer. Sawed-off. Really oughta buy one of those Snake Charmers, they'll blow your face right off. Elephant guns . . .

Okay. Where's the trigger? Look at that damn mutant. It's reaching for me! Covered all over in needles and teeth and claws. Get it in the arm! Bam!

Big thud. Heavy. Look, it has bones! No, must be wood. And it's bleeding. No, not blood, it's plant juice, sap, whatever. Slime. Water. On the ground. A pint's a pound the world around. On the ground.

·   ·   ·   ·   ·   ·   ·

wounded

·   ·   ·   ·   ·   ·   ·

Heavy.
So life is hard. Get a helmet.
Load. Get up close. Go for the middle. Blast her away! Take
    her out! Shoot!
Here it comes, falling, falling—jump!

omigod!
not pricks but stars----
you killed me

·   ·   ·   ·   ·   ·   ·

·   ·   ·   ·   ·   ·   ·

                    you killed me

·   ·   ·   ·   ·   ·   ·

·   ·   ·   ·   ·   ·   ·

sun   air   water   dirt   sky   time

·   ·   ·   ·   ·   ·   ·
·   ·   ·   ·   ·   ·   ·

VIII. The Maze

The basketmaker criss-crosses two strips of bear grass: north–south, east–west. She knots them, forming a precise center. Her old fingers are crooked and painful because she has woven baskets since time immemorial, as she puts it.

She's already gathered her materials. "I start by thanking the plants," she says, "and always leave some behind." Then she begins to coil the basket from the center, like a story from its "once upon a time." Glossy black fibers (devil's claw) stand out against pale green and white (yucca), yet the pattern does not spring perfectly clear until she stitches the last strand into the rim.

A small human figure stands at the entrance to a maze.

According to tradition, the whole cosmos centers around Baboquivari Peak, or Mountain Squeezed in the Middle, which towers over southwestern Arizona. The universe, desert, mountain, people, animals, plants, and all the rest were created long ago by I'itoi, Elder Brother. Pursued by enemies, I'itoi constructed just such a maze as this between the outside world and himself, and there he lives still, safe at the heart of Baboquivari. Anybody—enemy, fool, or holy person—may find a certain rocky cleft that leads to a cave on the western side of the mountain. But without the key to the maze, you will die, airless and thirsty, in the black passages underground.

The figure in the basket is, and is not, I'itoi. It also stands for every human being who faces life. Right choices lead to happiness ever after . . . the center of the basket.

She lays a bent forefinger on the passage closest to the human figure.

"I'm here," she smiles. "When I complete my circle I'll go to the center and rest in peace."

And the YouTube screen goes black.

The Road to Town

Rain fell on rain, on rain, on rain.

The last Pacific hurricane of the season had gone astray and soaked the deserts and mountains of New Mexico. The ranch roads were running like rivers, but the girl was wild to go to town.

"Will you drive me?" she begged her grandfather. "My parents won't do it."

"No," said the old man. "But I'll go with you."

"I don't know how to drive in all that mud," she objected.

"You've been driving on the ranch since you were six," he said.

"Not in mud. I hate mud!"

"Time you learned, then," said the grandfather.

She pouted. But twenty miles away in town there was a birthday party, and there was a boy, and she had just turned sixteen. Behind a long curtain of blue-black hair and a set of braces, she was partly pretty.

"Okay," she said. "If you'll coach me."

His old pickup truck was already thickly stuccoed with red dirt.

"I'm scared," she said.

"Me too." He had a face like a walnut shell, which split now into a slight smile. "Let's go anyway."

She started the engine.

"Take the old road," he said.

"New one's washed out?"

"Yep."

The truck crawled down the hill.

"So what's his name?" he asked.

"Granddad! Stop it!"

"Not too slow, not too fast," said the grandfather. "Steady. Keep moving. Yes, that's it."

The arroyo at the foot of the hill was running fast and deep.

"The bottom there is rocky," he said, "so you know you won't sink, don't you? Speed up and go right through. Don't stop."

The old ranch road did not run straight like the new one, but thanks to centuries of tamping by hooves and wheels, its surface was harder, and it was fairly flat. Neither road had ever been paved.

"This kind of day, this kind of drive brings back memories," the old man said.

"Why, Granddad?"

"Oh, it's a long story."

"Good," the girl said. "It's a long road."

"Always stay in the center if you can."

"Why?"

"Most roads are higher there, and drier. You don't want to slip into the ditch, right? And watch the tire tracks. Don't follow the deep sloppy ones."

The girl relaxed when she reached the county road, which was unpaved but wide enough for two cars to pass.

"Now you can tell me the story," she said.

"No, here's where you watch the road," said the grandfather. "Some parts are clay and some aren't. Remember where the school bus got stuck?"

For a mile or two, the only sounds in the cab of the truck were the loud splashes of tires, the occasional groans of the truck springs, and the tick and sweep of the windshield wipers.

"Good," said the old man. "Keep it up, just like that." He leaned back. "Well now, this road reminds me of a mining engineer I used to know."

"Like you. Before you came back to the ranch."

"That's right," he said. "It was a long time ago. This guy traveled the world. Some folks like to stay home and some don't."

I don't, thought the girl impatiently. *As soon as I can, I'm going.*

"Why'd you ever come back, Tata?" she asked, slipping into her childhood nickname for him.

He looked over at her with an expression that might seem blank on another face, but for him it betrayed surprise.

There was a small silver mine on the ranch, long worked out and abandoned, but in his boyhood, miners were still digging there. He had hung around until they let him sort the heavy rocks with fascinating glints in them from the other rocks. The ranch could only support a few people, so most of the family must find another way to make a living. Maybe he would find buried treasure.

After a moment he said, "The folks needed me on the ranch."

"But—"

"Slow down a little," said the grandfather. He did not want to talk to her about old age, horse accidents, bad years, or feelings.

"Okay."

But after a while he said: "Do you know what *querencia* means?"

"No."

"You will someday."

"Tell me."

But her grandfather said he'd have to think about it. He didn't know the word in English.

"Go on with the story, please, Tata."

"This guy," the old man said, "was the superintendent of a small gold mine in the Philippines."

"Gold? For real? You're not just teasing me?"

"The gold was real, what there was of it, but the job was pretty crummy. The mine was an hour's drive from the nearest town, but none of the workers lived there, including the superintendent. Everybody lived in town."

"Why?"

"Not safe."

Of course, he reflected, mines themselves were not safe either. Once, while climbing down a ladder in another mine in a different country, he had noticed that the carbide light in his helmet was fading and flickering. Bad air, he thought, and then the light went out. He just had time to throw his weight across the rungs before he passed out too.

All at once the road seemed to turn from sand to grease.

"Steer into the skid! Other way! Don't brake!"

"*You* drive!" the girl cried.

"Just go steady," her grandfather said. "You're doing fine."

"No, I'm not!"

But she drove on.

There must have been some oxygen in the bad air because eventually he came to and managed to clamber down the ladder and escape.

"That mine was unsafe," he continued, "especially at night, because there were headhunters in the jungle, or maybe bandits, or maybe guerrillas, or even maybe some guys doing three jobs at one time."

"Headhunters! Stop teasing, Tata."

"I'm not. There were headhunters. Supposed to be retired, but you never know."

"Wow," she said.

He shrugged. "Life's dangerous, *m'hijita*. Here on the border you have to keep your wits about you too. From the hilltops, from the shadows, the drug guys are watching us right now."

"Yeah," she said. "I know."

Yet to her they seemed almost as unreal as headhunters.

"You have your pistol under the seat," she said.

The old man shrugged and shook his head.

"Poor Rob Krentz," he said. "Never got a chance to shoot."

Last year a neighbor rancher had been murdered: it was a drug-related crime that would never be officially solved, even though the killer's identity was known.

"Mostly nothing happens," she suggested. That's why, she thought, I'm going to Paris, or New York, or even Las Cruces. Not Deming. Never Deming.

They bumped along in silence for several minutes before the old man spoke again.

"Mostly," he said, "you're lucky."

The girl agreed, not really understanding.

"Watch it!"

The old man grabbed the girl's arm with his harsh, dry hand, and just inches ahead of them a deer launched itself across the road. Its white tail flashed and it was gone. The girl froze.

"Stop! There's usually more than one."

And there were three.

"They come out when the light is low," her grandfather said, releasing her arm. "You know that. So do the mountain lions," he added wryly.

She took her foot off the brake and they moved on.

"Anyway," he said, "the superintendent made a rule that everybody had to go home before dark. The road to town wasn't safe at night either. But there came a day he broke his own rule."

Now their road began to climb a steep hill made up of shaky loose rocks and boulders.

"Set your tires on the big rocks," he instructed, "and go slow, or you'll get us high-centered."

"Tata! Should I use four-wheel drive?"

"Naaaww," he said as they hopped over the top. As they descended, scraggly mesquite trees began to replace the oaks and piñon pines of the highlands where the ranch headquarters was located. At the bottom of the slope, a stream seethed with broken branches and creamy globs of foam. "DO NOT ENTER WHEN FLOODED," warned a sign.

"Huh," said the old man. "Let's have a look."

Fresh tire tracks ran into the water and emerged on the other side.

"Follow the tracks?" asked the girl.

But he pulled off his boots and socks, rolled up his Wranglers, and waded in.

"Are you coming?" he asked.

"Why?"

"So you can tell how deep it is. And how solid the streambed is. And what's hiding underwater."

So now I'm going to get all wet and dirty, she thought glumly, but she followed him anyway, and although the rocks jabbed her bare feet, the water was clear and fairly shallow and there were no hidden hazards.

On the other side of the flood another long slope presented itself.

"Finish the story, Tata," urged the girl.

"Well," he said, "that day he forgot and worked till it was getting dark and raining and everyone else was gone. So he got in his Jeep."

"And—?"

"He came upon a car pulled off to the side of the road. A

man was sitting in it. On a country road it's always courteous to stop and help, but it was dusk and he was nervous, so he drove on by."

"Oh!"

"But then he felt guilty and turned around. And he discovered that the driver was slumped over the steering wheel with a fresh bullet hole in the middle of his forehead."

"Oh!"

"There's clay on this hill," her grandfather pointed out.

"Go on, go on!"

"He knew the murderer was probably watching him from the trees. He jumped in his Jeep—gunned it—slipped off the road—and got stuck. Watch out!"

The girl spun the steering wheel, but nonetheless the truck skidded over the edge of the road and landed in the ditch with a reverberating thump.

"Ay yi yi," remarked the old man.

"Oh, Tata!" she wailed. "I knew this would happen!"

"Don't spin your wheels," said her grandfather. "It never helps. Rock the truck back and forth, a little forward, a little back. Again. Stop."

"No good," said the girl despairingly and burst into tears.

"Aw, don't cry. There's a lot worse things, honey, like bullet holes in your head."

He got out and inspected all four wheels.

"Get me the shovel!" he called. "It's behind your seat."

For once, success came after just a few minutes of work. Back on the road again and not much muddier, the girl congratulated herself. I won't miss the party after all.

"So what did *he* do?" she asked.

"Just what we did. Put rocks under the tires and kept rocking."

Here they came to a sign that they passed so often that

they rarely read it anymore. But this time the grandfather looked at it.

CAUTION

PRIMITIVE ROAD

ILLEGAL ACTIVITIES AND SMUGGLING IN AREA

PROCEED AT YOUR OWN RISK

"Did you see something?" said the girl.

He shook his head. "Why did I ever come back?" he said. "Good question. Well, in spite of everything, this is my country. I know the shapes of all the hills."

"Pretty soon I'm going away to college."

"Yes," he said. "You are."

They drove on in silence. Finally he broke it.

"*Querencia* isn't home," he said.

"No?" she prompted.

"More like . . ."

"Love?"

His eye-slits narrowed a little. "I was going to say ache. Whatever makes birds go south."

"Tata! What happened to the superintendent?"

"He got away. At least . . . at first."

"Oh no!"

"Stay in the tracks," he reminded her. "Well, he drove as fast as he dared, but it got dark, and then he saw a pair of headlights."

She gasped.

"The headlights followed him all the way to town."

"But then he was okay?"

"No, because the car kept on following him. And it looked a hell of a lot like the car where he'd found the dead man. Watch out!"

She swerved around the first traffic they'd seen all day, another muddy truck.

"Sorry, Tata. What happened next?"

"Ah, here we are. Slow down. Speed limit's 25, remember."

"Yes—?"

"That town was small, like this one. He zigzagged, speeded, stopped, and started. Never looked back. Couldn't go home."

"No."

"Finally, he lost the guy. Or the guy lost him. Is this your friend's house?"

"Yes. But—but—is that all?

The old man smiled. "Not quite."

The girl bounced in her seat. "Go on!"

"Next day the car and the dead man were gone. No trace, no tracks. It'd rained all night, but he could still see the place where he got stuck. He felt very jumpy at first, but when nothing more ever happened, he wondered a little about the headlights and the chase."

"But the dead man was real."

"Sometimes," he said, "he wondered."

"Oh!"

"But then he would remember the smell. That must've been real. Burnt, human, blood, meat." He was silent for a moment. "Bad things happen, but I hope you never smell that."

Wide-eyed, the girl slid slowly down from the truck. She shook back the curtain of black hair, which now lit by weak sunlight reflected brilliant patches of pink and blue. She was thinking about the boy.

"I'll be back at four o'clock sharp."

She nodded. "Thanks, Granddad."

"Better not drive that road after dark."

"No."

Abruptly, all her awe and fear vanished. Her ill-assorted features joined in a broad smile, her braces flashed, and her grandfather caught a glimpse of the handsome adult she would someday be.

"We mustn't break the rule, must we?"

"Don't you be sassy, now."

"Next time, Granddad, tell me a story about *you*."

The old man jerked the truck into reverse and then looked down at her and once again allowed his walnut face to crack a little around the mouth. Deep in their slits his eyes seemed to be watering, as usual.

"*Ay, m'hijita,*" he said, "I just did."

The Frog Prince

A drop of blood.

It was the merest pink stain—a rosebud—but Teresa Slade stared at it in horror. Hairs prickled along the edge of her scalp. After a moment, she mechanically finished dressing and lay down on the bed. Teresa felt, or imagined she felt, a sensation of infinitesimal bubbles rising in her abdomen. Her hands and feet were cold.

"No," she said. "I refuse."

The child fell asleep, knees tucked up to her chin, pink fingers softly fisted. Suddenly they become aliens, Teresa thought, in orbit with the cherubim and seraphim.

> One to watch and one to pray
> And two to bear my soul away.

She turned her face to the Pacific. Late July light bashed the water. She had forgotten how seductive the ocean was. So much water: it would not be denied. Ray, who rarely spoke while driving, cleared his throat.

"How do you feel?" he said, his eyes on the road.

Like a morgue, thought Teresa.

"Fine." She kept her voice normal. "Fifty miles to go."

"Your first trip to San Diego," Ray said.

The air conditioner whirred while Teresa prepared her answer: "I've heard a lot about it."

And so the words came out, banal, effortless, true as far as they went. The moment passed. She sank back into her study of the ocean, but the lie continued to flavor her mouth. She'd only intended to leave an old love affair tactfully vague, but Ray had caught her off-guard again, as he had when he proposed this surprise vacation.

"Someplace new!" he said, with an eagerness that she hated to destroy.

After ten years of marriage, did any brief episode really matter? She shut her eyes against the glare.

At first the bleeding had stopped when she lay down. There was no pain. "This is not uncommon," said the doctor. Teresa willed messages to her body: keep, hold, save, be, then got up and went back to work. Every afternoon the clouds bloomed over the mountains, daring her to dream of summer rain, but by the time the evenings came, the clouds had blown away.

Now the ocean shrank into a blue trapezoid wedged between buildings, and plumes of bougainvillea dazzled the eye. The car jerked fitfully along in late afternoon traffic: blinding heat, then black shadows, but in the back seat the child continued to sleep.

"There's the bridge to Coronado Island," Ray said.

They sprang onto the bridge and spun along its curve. The harbor was full of frail sailboats. Teresa smelled the sea, bitter, salty, familiar as some bodily fluid, metallic, fishy, sweetly rotten. The substance chemically closest to seawater is blood.

She thought: You could slip through those steel barriers if you were slim . . . balance on the edge . . . cold water. . . . Teresa recoiled from the window. The car landed at the end of the bridge and was sucked onto the island.

"Where's the hotel?" she asked.

"Just let me drive," Ray said abruptly.

She turned away, throat burning with tears. They whipped past a little park; surely she saw a monkey in a cage surrounded by a lawn? Then she saw a young woman standing in a garden blowing bubbles all alone.

A murmur came from the back seat. From the moment of

conception Teresa had been certain it was a daughter and had named her "Claire."

"Where are we?"

"On an island," Teresa answered playfully.

The child peered out the window. "No. It's just a regular place."

"You and I and Daddy," said Teresa, "are in a car, on an island, in San Diego."

Claire pondered. "Where did Arizona go?"

"San Diego is in California. We live in another state."

These Chinese boxes of time and space were hard to explain.

> How many miles to Babylon?
> Threescore miles and ten.
> Can I get there by candlelight?
> Yes, and back again.

"Once upon a time" made sense; "last week" did not. "Someday, when you grow up" was meaningless. "Always," Teresa said to Claire. Or, "Never."

One summer night when Teresa was nineteen she lay on a grassy hilltop, stargazing.

Showing off, she said: "If the earth is in the solar system, and the solar system is in the Milky Way, and the Milky Way is in space, where's space?"

Michael did not respond. She pressed on, teasing him.

"Say space is curved. Infinite. What's beyond the curve?"

"Stop it!"

"What's the matter?"

"Don't," he said.

"Don't what?"

"I don't want to hear it," Michael said, in real distress.

"But, Michael, you believe in science, don't you?"

They were lying side by side at the top of a slope. Suddenly, he seized her tightly and rolled them both over the edge. Like a log, like children, like the victims of an accident, like lovers, they went tumbling down the hill.

"Oh joy!" she said at the bottom.

"Good," said Michael's voice in the dark.

Ray braked, and a shower of small plastic toys fell from the back seat to the floor. "That's the Del Coronado Hotel," he said.

Claire called out, "It's a castle!"

It was an enormous red cone encircled by ring after ring of white dormer windows, ending in a frivolous little turret topped off by a red dunce cap flying an American flag.

"It looks like Stanford," Teresa said.

"Built about the same time," Ray said.

A white Rolls Royce nudged around them.

"Ray, can we afford this?"

He accelerated behind the Rolls. More toys tumbled off the back seat.

"We need a change," he said, and went to register.

"Mommy, where are we?"

"Soon we'll go to the beach," said Teresa.

"Beach?"

A young Japanese woman climbed the stairs to the hotel lobby, her cap of straight hair and her yellow silk dress belling out with each step. When she reached the top, she turned sideways and gazed searchingly behind her. Teresa saw that she was pregnant.

"Teresa?" Ray slipped a heavy brass key into her hand. "I'll find a bellman."

Along a path lined with flowering shrubs, men in formal dress rolled loaded carts shrouded in pink linen. Waiters.

She opened the car door and felt the ocean in the air. With Claire's hand in hers, Teresa followed Ray and the bellman into the antique elevator. A golden arrow indicated the number of the floor.

"It reminds me," Teresa whispered.

"Rome," said Ray.

"The gnome of Rome," said Teresa.

As students, they creaked up to their cheap *pensione* in an iron cage so small and jerky that passengers constantly fell into one another's arms. The gnome greeted them kindly at the top. Bent nearly double by age, disease, or some wicked spell, he hobbled about the *pensione*, sometimes carrying clean coarse sheets, sometimes platters of spaghetti.

The carpet was striped with sunlight; the bellman unlocked a louvered door.

"This seems familiar too," she said.

"There's something odd about the room," Ray said, "but on short notice, it's the best I could do."

Teresa stepped across the threshold and began to laugh a little too loudly. Ray tipped the bellman and shot her a glance.

"No, no," she said. "It's fine. It's lovely. It's like the Three Bears. Besides, right now it doesn't matter, does it?"

The room was pie-shaped—a slice of a tower—with flowered wallpaper and old-fashioned furniture. In a row against the wall stood three single beds.

"Dibs!" cried Teresa and sat on the first bed. Pain spiraled up the center of her body.

"Are you all right?" he asked.

"Just fine."

"Lie back," Ray said roughly, and she obeyed.

"Look!" She pointed out the window. "Stanford again."

Geometric red roof sections filled the frame.

"Inner Quad," Teresa babbled on. "Memorial Church. No,

Mem Chu before the earthquake—the first earthquake, I mean. When the ceiling was still covered by a giant painting of the Eye of God."

She wondered what they'd missed by skipping their tenth reunion. Her old roommate reported that women looked better (more expensive clothes) but men worse (less hair). Everyone used to speak sarcastically of "Stanford marriages," bound to end badly. But we made them anyway, Teresa thought. The pattern of her life since college was like a drawing that began with a few lines and grew dense with detail. Degrees, careers, why should she feel that anything was missing? It was irrational. Nobody had a perfect life. The single bed felt as narrow as a diving board.

"This is from an early advertisement," Teresa said and read aloud: "Numerous tourists who visit this charming place must see visions of matrimonial bliss, past or present, real or imaginary, when they enter its portals, for it is a favorite resort for the newly wedded, when love supreme shines out upon a beautiful world."

Ray rolled his eyes, but she went perversely on: "Even the varied sounds of Old Ocean are attuned to this theme. Ah! It is a divine gift to be young and in love; but thrice happy he, she, who, through the magic of imagination can recreate the happy past and live again in memory. Such happiness comes to those who yield to the prevailing spirit of Hotel del Coronado . . ."

Ray walked to the window. "No ocean view," he said. "Where's the beach?"

"In a minute or two," said Teresa, "we'll go and find it."

The black blood had escaped slowly, trace after trace.

"All we can do is wait," said the doctor. "I suppose you ought to go to bed."

Teresa stared at the ceiling, afraid to move, afraid to admit to a small steady flicker of pain. Those bubbles below her navel, however, continued for days. She lay there for a week while her work and household fell into disarray. Hour after hour she watched the sun weigh down the landscape outside.

"Don't worry, Claire," she said from time to time. "It'll be all right."

Dusk was falling when the Slades reached the beach, deserted except for a middle-aged jogger. The tide was out. Claire looked at the empty white sand, threw herself down, and rolled in ecstasy like a puppy. She tagged after her parents as they followed the tideline, marked by heaps of kelp.

Ray said, "Since there's no beach at home, let's come here every day."

Teresa nodded. The sleek brown kelp was fouled with plastic fishing line.

Ray enclosed her chilled hand in his hot and sticky one. "Every day we'll also do something different—drive around, go to the zoo."

"I think I'm hungry now," said Teresa.

They were almost the only diners in the Crown Room, a sort of overturned ship. The wooden ceiling curved two stories above their table with its watery circle of candlelight, and there was little on the formal menu to appeal to a child.

"Vichyssoise," said Teresa. Potato soup should be safe, she thought, comforting. But it arrived in a silver bowl embedded in cracked ice and garnished with snipped chives.

"According to the brochure, the original hotel was built in 1888," Teresa tasted the soup. "So you were right about the date."

"Le-land-Stan-ford-Jun-ior-U-niversity—" Ray intoned, deadpan.

"Or-ganized-1891." Teresa finished the cheer. "Yes!"

Their eyes met. She remembered sitting beside him in the cavernous old football stadium while on the field far below the Stanford band marched in their underwear, bawdy, rowdy, and intensely self-conscious about it. Once when they were still almost strangers, Ray amazed her by confessing that he was very shy. "I hate to stand up and yell, 'Hey, Pepsi man!'"

No other bid from him to her would ever be quite so surprisingly intimate, and once accepted, it opened the way to all the rest. He was a tall man with heavy muscles in his arms and shoulders, and in the dim light he might pass either for twenty or forty.

"You should eat more than that," he said.

"I'm fine. The brochure also said that this is where the Prince of Wales first met Wallis Simpson."

"Oh?"

There was even a photograph. The dolly prince, his outer surface apparently painted on and varnished, leaned an ear toward a talking woman wearing a lavish bundle of hair. But the woman in the picture was unidentified, not the future Duchess of Windsor, merely a "Coronado housewife" at the time—one of a thousand guests at a reception in the Grand Ballroom.

"1920," said Teresa.

"Nothing in California is really old," said Ray.

Michael laughed in genuine amusement at the idea of going to a museum.

Propped on one elbow, he threw back his head, and Teresa saw that his teeth were completely white. Sand clung to his wet arms and legs as though he had been sugared.

"Isn't that a terrible waste of time?" he asked.

A waiter attempted to remove the vichyssoise.

"Not yet," Teresa said.

Ray moved a slice of his steak to her plate.

"You know I don't like rare!" But Teresa bit back the words and sat quietly while red juices oozed into her bread, leaving a pink stain. She heard the clink of metal against china, the ping of glassware, hushed adult voices, and, faintly, the roar and whisper of the ocean.

"Tell me about the handsome prince," said Ray.

"Oh, he was dull and stupid, really."

"Didn't they elope, or something?"

"Yes, but that was later. Husbands later." She drank her wine and felt its effect: not an improvement, but a welcome change. Ray refilled her glass, and she smiled.

"Then Marilyn Monroe made a movie here."

"After the prince left?"

"He was just a wandering duke by then."

"Which movie?"

"*Some Like It Hot.*"

"I don't remember it," said Ray, and she felt his attention lapse.

"Am I boring you?"

"No, I was just thinking about work. Sorry."

Teresa struggled and said brightly, "It's all a matter of profit and loss really."

"Even Marilyn Monroe and the prince? What about 'happily ever after'?"

"This is it." She wiped her lips.

> First comes love
> Then comes marriage
> Then comes someone with a baby carriage.

The Slades moved through the lobby without haste, observing other guests and architectural details.

"'One of the largest wooden structures in the world,'"

Teresa quoted from the brochure, and suddenly she was weary. "Bedtime," she said.

Sleepy Claire drooped, a dead weight, over her shoulder. There was another youngish couple in the elevator; the woman held a toddler in her arms. The elevator operator rasped in a voice full of venom: "I say make 'em walk. Never carry 'em if they can walk."

It was a relief to escape and to lock the door behind them. How quickly we set up housekeeping, Teresa thought, as they began the bedtime rituals. She sat down cautiously—less pain. As far as she knew, Michael still lived here.

Ray reached across from his bed. "You seem a long way off."

"It's like being in the hospital."

"No," he said. "Not much."

She closed her eyes. The cusp of consciousness was the worst time. Toads hopped out of the darkness. Divers entangled themselves in forests of kelp. She had committed a misdeed, a failure, a blunder, a crime. She could not not think of it. Blood. Suspended within the hollow wooden hive of the hotel she floated, hollow herself as a blown eggshell.

> Neither fish, flesh, fowl, nor bone,
> I kept it till it ran alone.

As they were leaving the room the next morning Teresa discovered that she'd lost her key.

"I gave it to you yesterday when we checked in," Ray said.

"I know. But it's not in my purse."

"Maybe you dropped it in the car."

A light fog hung over the ocean, the color of steel and nearly flat. Chasing Claire past the tennis courts, Teresa overheard a man criticizing his doubles partner's last shot. The woman twirled her racket and smiled tightly.

The Slades unfurled their towels on the beach. Overnight the dry sand had been raked into a tidy pattern that half-buried the cigarette butts. The ocean had an icy bite; they waded once and turned back. Claire seemed fearful of the surf. Her small, cold fingers clutched and dragged at Teresa's wet legs. But she was content to play in the sand while Ray and Teresa observed the scene. As soon as the fog burned off, bright rented umbrellas popped up, older children played paddleball, swimmers strode into the water, a young woman undressed adroitly beneath a towel. Boats materialized on the horizon. All the while a succession of airplanes buzzed the beach and landed somewhere just out of sight.

"Navy planes," said Ray.

"Like a war zone."

"San Diego's full of Navy—sailors, Marines, divers. Have you had enough of this?"

"No, I'm going to get wet. Too cold for you?"

"Be careful," he said.

"I'm really fine, you know," Teresa said.

"They warned us about dangerous currents," he said.

> Mother, may I go out to swim?
> Yes, my darling daughter.
> Hang your clothes on a hickory limb
> And don't go near the water.

Teresa gasped as the seawater smacked her abdomen, but when she dived through a wave and began to swim she felt peculiarly alive.

During the summer before she met Ray, Michael taught her to scuba dive. He was a half-hearted oceanography student up from San Diego State who found the Bay Area cold and boring. Just as a casual experiment (she felt sure) one day he seized and kissed her. She could still call up the light and the wind of that day, the crush, the glow and the blow of it, the crunch of bones, the body temperature, the perfect fit.

One night in Italy, trespassing in the dark, Teresa stole an apple off a gnarled tree no taller than herself. The apple was the size of a big cherry yet fully ripe and she ate it core, seeds, and all. It was the ultimate of appleness. She never told Ray. Nothing to share with anyone.

The Hotel del Coronado included an arcade of glittering boutiques selling pint flasks of Joy perfume. Framed hotel memorabilia hung upon the walls among the shops, and Teresa paused at a photograph of Marilyn Monroe and Jack Lemmon facing each other on the white beach. She wore a terrycloth robe as cottony as her hair, but he was dressed as a woman. *Some Like It Hot.*

"I have seen this place before," she said. "In black and white."

Ray nodded absently. Claire escaped into a shop.

"Look at the doll, Mommy!"

She stood upon a glass shelf, draped in a scanty white satin costume from some other movie. With colorless hair, heavy eyes, and mouth like a smear of raspberry jam, the small head was quite a good likeness,

"She's a Madame Alexander doll," said the clerk, protectively. "A collector's item."

Teresa read the three-digit price tag from where she stood.

"Come on, sweetie."

The Marilyn Monroe figure made Teresa remember her childhood. Other girls had bride dolls but she'd never owned one. Rag dolls, yes, and baby dolls that drank and wet and cried, and dolls with tiny clothes that you could change, but with a bride, there was only the wedding.

The movie came back. The girlish voice breathed: "Ooh! I'm not very bright."

"Does it come with a little toy pill bottle?" asked Ray, suddenly behind her.

She was angry all the way to the car. But when her room key was not there, the balance of power shifted.

"I'm sorry. I can't understand what happened."

"Maybe you dropped it on the ground."

The palm trees leaned at silly angles like Dr. Seuss characters.

"Are we too old to go to the zoo?" said Ray.

Teresa said no, it was world-famous, just look at all those flamingos. They strolled from birds to monkeys. A troop of little screaming primates flung themselves in fits of frustration from one side of their enclosure to the other. High on an artificial treetop she saw a female with an infant clamped to her hairy chest.

> When the bough breaks
> The cradle will fall

The Slades walked slowly, Claire's pace. In the middle of the day the weather was extremely hot and dry, so babies were taking siestas in their strollers, their big heads in grotesque slumps. Teresa averted her eyes from the unbearable sadness of the gorillas. The elephants and giraffes stood patiently under the sun; the lions were lost in sleep. The Slades followed a shadowy path through a mock rain forest and emerged into the glare near the entrance of the zoo. A river of families meandered past. Obese, red-faced parents tugged and slapped at their skinny-legged offspring; grandparents beamed and picked their teeth. Teresa watched freckled children gather around a freckled mother in a maternity dress.

"Heredity," Ray said lightly. He steered her toward the exit. "Let's not dine with the prince tonight. I thought he was a goddamn gloomy guy."

They chose a restaurant on top of a cliff in La Jolla.

"You should always eat fresh fish beside the ocean," Ray

said. "Ha. Look at that, will you? Maine lobster. Alaskan king crab."

"Abalone," Teresa pointed out. "That's from California."

Web-footed Michael tramped out of the surf, black and earless in his diving gear, gripping one rocky object in each glove. She built a little fire on the beach. Deftly, he broke into the shells, sliced up the quivering mollusks, and tossed them into a pan with butter and garlic.

"Aren't they rubbery?" asked Ray.

"If you just barely cook them, they're wonderful."

"Still—look at the price."

"They must have gotten scarce," she said.

Through the restaurant window they saw the lights of boats out in the water and a few dim stars overhead. The woman at the next table described a storm.

"Incredible waves! This place was just totally flooded. There were like tables floating! Awesome! Waves reached up into the parking lot. A woman was swept away!"

"Unreal," said the woman's escort.

Ray's eyebrows went up.

"This puts me in the mood for Sea World," he said.

Teresa managed to laugh. Later, the parking lot looked as safe and dry as any other. There was no storm, no wind, no rain, although they could hear the ocean hissing at the foot of the cliff down below. At the hotel she searched her purse for the key again without success. While Ray was in the shower she clicked Google to "Diving San Diego." No danger in that, nothing to explain. She found Michael's advertisement almost immediately:

Oceanographic Consultants

Marine Construction & Repair
Underwater Salvage

She heard Ray coming and she exited Google.

Michael rented a boat for the final dive and took the class to sea. When at last the moment came to jump, Teresa wavered, so he gave her a push. Falling, she lost track of her mouthpiece, breathed seawater, tried to come up, forgot to allow for the weight belt, and panicked. After one gasp on the surface she sank again in disbelief. She was a strong swimmer; she could never drown. Finally, Michael, trailing a scarf of silver bubbles, pulled and shoved her into the bottom of the boat, retching and shivering uncontrollably. After a long warm embrace he said, "You flunk."

> Down by the seashore,
> Down by the sea

"By the sea, by the sea, by the beautiful sea," sang Marilyn Monroe. Her black chiffon gown veiled her fat white flesh. In *Some Like It Hot* her character's name was Sugar. Sugar was a sucker for shady saxophone players, although she claimed she wanted to marry a millionaire. Bubbles drifted past her face as she gasped out her song: "You and me, you and me, how happy we'll be. . . ."

This time the Slades discovered an elaborate sand castle on the beach. Claire did not touch it until a little boy came by. The two children locked gazes. Then they both gleefully rushed at the castle and trampled it. When its grown-up builders came along, they were indignant.

"So much work, gone!"

"How could anyone do such a thing?"

The Slades pulled their hats over their faces and lay still.

At the end of the summer Michael and Teresa walked along a beach together. A north wind blew at San Gregorio, sending sea foam scudding across the wet sand, so they searched for a sheltered place. Then Michael turned and spoke.

"You're standing on love."

"What?"

At their feet someone had sculpted a row of raised letters, so large that she'd failed to see the pattern, and the toe of her shoe had already disturbed the "L." But "O," "V," and "E" were still in perfect condition.

Teresa woke the next morning bruised, with salty lips, sand in her scalp, and the scent of seaweed in her nostrils.

Sea World was more like a circus than a zoo. First, the seals lumbered through their tricks, then, sleek in their neoprene skins, humans performed rodeo stunts astride the killer whales. The penguins perched on mounds of artificial snow and stared gravely through glass at the air-conditioned tourists. Teresa purchased a handful of limp minnows for Claire to feed to a walrus but ended up dropping them one by one into the tank herself. The creature watched them as they sank, and at the last possible moment it opened its whiskery jaws.

"The original mermaid," said Ray.

Teresa leaned over the rail at the shark pond. They were trim, taut and stylish, terrible and seductive.

"Somehow," she said, "they remind me of the Duchess of Windsor."

"Poor little rich guy."

"The little man on the wedding cake."

The sharks swam in figure eights and flashed their fins. Ray whistled.

"Definitely not Marilyn Monroe."

Fame, money and all those men, Teresa thought. No children.

Sea World teemed with children. Some strained on leashes, some were babes in arms. Monstrously crippled ones rode in wheelchairs. Others jostled through the crowds, squealing and stepping on toes. Teresa lifted Claire up to see a school of silver fishes move all of a piece, like a siren undulating in a sequined gown.

> One for sorrow, two for joy,
> Three for a girl, four for a boy.
> Five for silver, six for gold,
> Seven for a secret ne'er to be told.

All at once she was afraid she was going to cry.

"We need to go!" she said.

Teresa lay for half the night with open eyes. She watched electric snake tongues dart through the blackness on the edge of the world. Heat lightning. But no rain.

A mashed strawberry. A blood clot. A red-hot measuring tape encircling her waist. More blood, bits of raw meat, then a ball of blood. And it was over except for mopping.

"You mustn't blame yourself," said the doctor.

She told him about the tiny bubbles she had felt below her navel.

"No, no," he said. "You couldn't have. Too early. Put it out of your mind."

He muttered to Ray, man to man: "Hemorrhage . . . few days' rest . . . maybe a little bit blue."

> There was an old woman
> And nothing she had,
> So this old woman
> Was said to be mad.

Teresa had left her hat at Sea World.

"Oh, well," said Ray, shutting the door behind them.

"Shouldn't you put on the chain? There's a lost key out there. Anyone could come in."

He stretched calmly on his bed to read the *Wall Street Journal*. Teresa lay on hers. In a way she was surprised that Michael owned a business, for after school started he had written her a single letter from San Diego containing four misspelled words. Marine salvage, she thought. Did that mean sunken treasure or dead bodies? She began to compose a letter in her head: "Should I look up my old flame? Should I seek out my natural parents? Should I tell my husband everything?"

"Shall we try it?" Michael whispered in her ear. "Just to see if it works?"

What a marvelous joke! Laughing, she dug her fingers into his back muscles.

> There was a man of double deed
> Sowed his garden full of seed.
> When the seed began to grow
> 'Twas like a garden full of snow.

"You've been asleep," said Ray.

Teresa felt numb and gray, as though she had been poisoned. Claire curled close beside her.

"I didn't want to leave you," he went on. "But now I'm going downstairs to buy a thriller."

When the door closed behind him, she reached for her computer and found the name. But instead of "Michael," the listing read "Michael and Bernadette."

Later that evening, she worked it casually into the conversation: "You know, I actually have been here before." Ray looked mildly surprised. Quickly she went on. "I landed at the airport once."

"On your way to somewhere else?"

"Yes."

"Well, that hardly counts, does it?"

Teresa's mistake was clear the moment she saw Michael at the airport. Not recognizing her, he lounged against a railing. His face was as beautiful as ever, but he was chewing gum, and he looked both lustful and sullen.

> He loves me,
> He don't,
> He'll have me,
> He won't,
> He would
> If he could,
> But he can't
> So he don't.

He hardly protested at all when she caught the next flight back to San Francisco.

Ray breathed evenly; Teresa could not sleep. Light and shade flickered before her eyes, bringing back Dr. Alvarez Tostado, her astronomy professor, as he operated his orrery in a darkened lecture hall.

"It is an astronomical instrument," he explained. "It illustrates by the revolution of balls the motions of the solar system. Mercury, Venus, Earth, Mars, Jupiter, Saturn, Uranus, Neptune, Pluto."

Shadows flitted across the screen, then vanished when he turned on the lights. Here and there among the students, young men were found to be sleeping. Plenty of other fish in the sea. Scuba divers waddled into the surf, hand in hand. The buddy system. Young men marched in their underwear, in the shadow of red, penile Hoover Tower. She often wondered what fool or joker had designed such a structure for a college campus. The black bars around the top were added later: suicide prevention. She rolled over. The medical textbook had not helped: "This event is rarely accepted with equanimity by the patient and her family. The patient may lose a considerable amount of blood . . ."

And a hat, a key, virginity, a golden opportunity, burgled treasures, a head of hair, a waist, a taste, a train, a plane, a ship, a patient, a button, a wallet, a fortune, a job, a race, your mind, your wife, your faith, your life.

> Lucy Locket lost her pocket,
> Kitty Fisher found it;
> There was not a penny in it,
> But a ribbon round it.

The beach had been manicured during the night, and more military planes roared across the sky. Teresa extended her arms and legs in the sand. Sunlight poured upon her boggy midsection, but she still felt cold and old and gray.

"Why are you so unhappy?" Ray asked. "Isn't this enough? Aren't I enough?"

"I'm going to swim," she told him.

"I'll be right here," he answered.

He watched as she walked toward the water. She waded in up to her knees and paused as the waves sucked sand from underneath her feet. Other bathers splashed nearby; children shrieked. Then all at once Teresa heard another sound above the rhythm of the sea.

Beyond the breakers, men's voices were chanting. She strained her ears to catch the words of their song, but she could not quite understand. When she shaded her eyes from the glare, she could barely see a group of dark heads bobbing just offshore in the shining water. The sound was rich and strange. She listened in delight as they finished one song and began another.

"Mommy?"

Teresa turned and saw Claire, waist-deep.

"What are you doing, Mommy?"

"Hear the men singing?" Teresa said.

"Mommy, what's under the water?"

"More water."

Claire came closer, deeper. The ocean rocked unevenly about her.

"What's under that?"

"More and more and more. It's very deep."

"And then under that?"

"Rock. Dark. Hot, cold. Nothing. I don't know."

Some like it cold.

The child swayed up to her neck in the surf. The next good wave would sink her, Teresa realized. But she felt too numb to move.

"Where's home?" asked Claire. "Over there," said Teresa. She'd better start swimming to warm up. She was a strong swimmer. Could she reach those singers?

"Daddy says to come back."

Teresa half turned toward the beach, and she saw that Ray had risen to his feet. He stood far off at the edge of the water, pale and nearly naked, wordless, terrified.

> I had a little husband
> No bigger than my thumb.

"One I love," lisped Claire, "two I love . . . ."

> Three I love, I say,
> Four I love with all my heart,
> Five I cast away. . . .

The child floated between them, surrounded by patches of foam. My flesh and blood, thought Teresa. And his.

The song ended. The voices were gone.

Teresa took a last look out to sea, but the Navy frogmen

had dived beneath the surface. There was only the sound of the ocean now. Rich vaporous clouds formed cliffs and terraces in the bitter sky above. A strand of kelp slithered around her ankle. Teresa shuddered as she moved through the dark water and bumped finally into her husband's cold bare chest. Claire was gone, too.

Captain Death

Just before five o'clock on the morning of March 30, 2015, five Border Patrol agents spilled from their Chevy Suburban and went thudding toward the black mesquite thickets. Their bulletproof vests, boots, wires, flashlights, guns, and fat held them to a fast waddle, but the civilian who followed them was light on his feet.

"You! Jim!" one agent barked. "You stay here!"

James Zuckerman opened his mouth to shout, "NO."

Then he heard the ack-ack-ack-ack of an automatic weapon not far away, and his feet slowed down. If he must be martyred for journalism, he wanted something better than this: either to die while exposing a great atrocity, or to vaporize into a stinking pink cloud in a real war zone, preferably with his murder captured for all time in an execution video. Not here in a damn quagmire with some redneck morons in cowboy hats.

Helmets for *them* would be a waste of good Kevlar, Zuckerman thought bitterly. They were still scuffling loudly through the brush, although any reasonably fleet smuggler within earshot must be long gone into the dawn. Mexico lay only a few hundred yards away, just across the Rio Grande.

Enjoying his poisonous mood, he stomped back to the Suburban. He hated to take orders. Disobedience was his creed. And now, finally, at the end of a sleepless, deadhead night shift, there was action: a tip came in, and off they went. He would probably miss everything, perhaps something shocking or brutal, really worth writing about, and that was very bad because at the moment his project was floundering. Still, around these idiots friendly fire was a real possibility.

Zuckerman was not and never would be a "Jim." Back in his newspaper days the old reporters had given him the only nickname he ever liked: Captain Death. He was fresh then, taking a juicy glee in journalism that he never felt now. But he soon left newspapers far behind, widening his scope to magazines, books, and broadcasting, and then he moved on to a full range of modern media. When he was Captain Death he'd covered little homicides and cheap corruption, but now it was global catastrophes. He delved deep into them and came back full of truth and blame. If those rednecks ever read anything but beer cans they would recognize his name.

Zuckerman had a big handsome head with curly hair and curly eyebrows that overhung sharp eyes set deep in sooty sockets. He moved with a certain swagger and down to the waist he possessed a linebacker's body, but since his legs were short, so was he. Lovely long-legged women never seemed to care.

"I can work while I wait," he said to himself.

Nap? Him? At 5:07 A.M.? Impossible.

Over the past few months he had traveled the Mexican border from California to this godforsaken tip of Texas, amassing data and interviewing all the way. He had burned through his publisher's advance, but to Zuckerman's increasing alarm no clarity had yet emerged in his mind. He'd watched tiny heads bob northward through the surf and past an ineffective barrier that stretched into the Pacific. He'd crawled through a drug-smuggling burrow that linked the twin towns of Mexicali and Calexico, and then, a few days later, in broad daylight, he'd witnessed two men scale the twenty-foot fence that separated Nogales, Sonora, from Nogales, Arizona, and instantly vanish into the shabby American streets.

It was clearly impossible to "secure" the border. Some areas remained totally unfenced, some short sections of fence were freestanding like outdoor sculpture, but most of the rest was easy to climb or step over, or to go around, or to dig under.

Virtual electronic walls were also full of virtual holes. Walls never worked, anyway, thought Zuckerman, except as a place to paint bilingual obscenities.

Something about a barrier made people want to break it down and cross it. *He* certainly did. Probably human beings were genetically driven to colonize the world just like bacteria. And humans were also the slaves of fantasy, an uncontrollable force that turned El Norte into El Dorado, while the reverse fantasy was equally potent: the War of the Worlds is upon us. And then there were drugs. Although Zuckerman was trying to ignore them and focus on immigration, drug tentacles writhed their way into everything.

Before he began, he'd boasted that all previous attempts to write about the border were the same old story in different words, muddled and shallow, reaching no real conclusions, but he, James Zuckerman, would get to the heart of it. Yet now he could not "see his way in."

In this carefully careless way he liked to describe his creative process to lecture audiences and journalism students. Before the border project, the magic always worked: he happily bushwhacked trails through wildernesses. Nuclear disaster? Cold fusion? Serial killer? Cancer cluster? North Korea? He slithered and slashed his way into the heart of them all. Why not now? It was one more story of human crime and doom. Poor Mexico, so far from God, so close to three hundred million gringos! Here on the border the third world smashed against the first world and bled.

And . . . the Suburban was locked, with all his gear inside. Including his cell phone, which must have slipped out of his pocket. Left in the dark! Zuckerman pounded futilely on the door, and then he gave the left rear tire a savage kick, regretting that the tire was not a certain book reviewer, a condescending troll who really could use a kick or two. "Zuckerman bites off more than he can chew," he wrote, "but he tries to chew it anyway." What if the troll was right? What if more trolls joined the chorus?

Zuckerman decided to break a window. What could they do to him? He would blame it on smugglers, but as he looked around the dank clearing for a rock, the twilight revealed nothing but mud. And garbage. So far, if his border book had a theme, that was it: plastic bottles, soup cans, amphetamine packets, old sneakers, paper bags, filthy underpants, human waste, and worse. Nobody would notice a pile of broken glass. Then, in a place where the mud looked trampled, something glinted. Probably more trash, he thought. He squatted down anyway and stood up with a dirty cell phone in his hand.

"Huh," Zuckerman said to himself. If not ruined, surely it was dead? But when he wiped the mud from the screen and thumbed the power button, to his great amazement the phone lit right up. It was unlocked, too, for he found himself reading text messages from earlier that same night. The phone belonged to someone named Alex and the message was recent.

MARCH 30, 2015

Dustin to Alex 12:42AM
???

Dustin 12:37AM
Txt me

Dustin 12:33AM
R u ok

Dustin 12:33AM
Bro

Dustin 12:30AM
Wasup

But of course this was the end, not the beginning. If read from top to bottom, the conversation would run backward, wouldn't it? So Zuckerman scrolled down to the earliest message he could find, which was dated five days ago, and read up from there.

MARCH 15, 2015

Alex to Jazmín 7:11PM
Can you talk
Boys 10 and 12

Jazmín 7:15PM
Where r they from n where r the parents

Alex 7:18PM
They are from Oaxaca their parents are going to pick them up from Houston

Jazmín 7:19PM
For when

Alex 7:20PM
Right now they just want a price

Jazmín 7:22PM
2000

Alex 7:29PM
Each right?

Jazmín 7:30PM
Of course. Half down half on delivery

Alex 7:30PM
Lol

Jazmín 7:31PM
Si

Kid smugglers! Zuckerman didn't have kids and didn't much like them, but he'd just toured a shelter in west Texas, a large cage with a concrete floor packed with undocumented minors all rolled up in silver space blankets like baked potatoes. Their captors seemed not to know what the hell to do, other than cage the kids and let them watch TV, although of course the young potatoes would eventually join their undocumented relatives from Maine to California. Perhaps some might see it as a crazy black farce, but James Zuckerman had too much gravitas to be a comic writer.

Zuckerman's mental chaos worsened when he tried to unravel causes and effects. For God's sake, $2000 would charter each kid a private plane. Desperation must drive parents to ship their children off like freight, yet those parents should bear some blame too. But what about those parents who sent their children out of Nazi Germany to protect them? Was this any different?

A memory jolted him: white bones sprawled on white New Mexico sand. Scraps of clothes and tufts of long black hair suggested that these were the remains of a young woman, but most of her smaller bones seemed to have vanished. Long ago Zuckerman had learned to view horror simply as subject matter, and this sunny skeleton was not the worst he'd ever seen. Later he would write about it coolly. So why, now, did he feel sick?

The sheriff's deputy cleared his throat. "Coyotes," he said.

Looking away, Zuckerman identified finger bones scattered like dice beneath a bush.

"If they can't keep up, they get left behind. Poor kid." The deputy bent over the bones. "Here's a pocket . . . sometimes they have I.D. Once," he added conversationally, "I even found a Chinese passport." He fumbled in the fraying denim and extracted something. "Ana Claudia Villa Herrera," he read aloud.

"*If* that's her real name!" snapped Zuckerman.

There he'd failed. Doubt everything, always, but never show emotion. And to be fair, not every law officer Zuckerman had ever met was a villain or a dunce. He nourished other and stronger hates, such as his rage at that religious group in Arizona who forced him to watch them "bless their fleet" of trucks that delivered water to immigrant trails in the desert. Did anybody drink it? Did it save lives? Did the bottles become litter? Maybe he was too hung up on garbage, but were there any solid facts here? No. But the truck-blessers felt good. To Zuckerman, anything eerie or irrational, especially religion, stank like cat food: he didn't want it to defile him.

But now, standing beside the Suburban deep in south Texas, he had forgotten Ana Claudia Villa Herrera because perhaps at last he'd glimpsed a trail through the mental badlands. *Was* garbage his theme? Of course the border was also an ecological disaster zone. "The trashing of the border country," he said experimentally to himself. He could track down the Center for Biological Diversity in Tucson and interview them too, balancing zealots against zealots. But then his excitement faded. No, it was no good. The idea itself was garbage.

I will not think about that paper bag, he thought, I will not, those things never bother me, why should that, and he continued to scroll through the messages. Jazmín was definitely Alex's boss.

MARCH 17, 2015

> **Jazmín** 3:04PM
> Did u get em

Alex 3:04PM
Yes ma they are all with me having bbq

> **Jazmín** 3:05PM
> R u gona take em tomorrow

Alex 9:24PM
Si ma

                                             Jazmín 9:53PM
Theres food sodas n water at the house

Alex 9:53PM
OK

MARCH 18, 2015

Alex 5:30AM
Kids safe in a motel until morning. I'll take them
to Houston myself but they are already in the
other side and safe ;)

                                             Jazmín 7:14AM
I will pay you the rest once I get the money

Alex 10:18AM
 I found a good car for 2 o clock. Don't
worry everything is under control

                                             Jazmín 10:21AM
Buy em burritos or corndogs at stripes they r
only fifty cents

Alex 10:21AM
OK mami

Ma? Mami? Could Jazmín possibly be Alex's *mother*? No, no, it
must be slang or bastard Spanish, not that there wasn't plenty
of bastard English too, in this goddamn lawless bastard border no man's land. "The border is a zone, not a line," people
told him, and it was true. A polluted, infected zone.

    Ma. He remembered his own mother, Alma Zuckerman,
standing proudly in front of shelf upon shelf of sugar bowls.

Silver, china, brass, plastic. Camels, cottages, cows, cats, cabbages, and the two stars of her collection: a giant hollow tooth and a tiny toilet bowl. "'Zucker' means sugar, you know," she never tired of repeating, nor he of retorting that sugar was the antithesis of all the Zuckermans he'd ever known, which actually was not many, although his father did have his own fine collection of old Zuckerman family stories about hairbreadth escapes from Nazis and unstoppable success in America.

The sugar bowls were all empty, of course. Alma herself preferred artificial sweeteners.

MARCH 18, 2015

Alex 1:34PM
Got 2 more ppl to cross tonight. Lets hold kids n
take em all to Houston manana

Jazmín 1:42PM
NO

Jazmín 1:42PM
Call me back rite now

Jazmín 2:47PM
Asshole where are u

Alex 8:28PM
At checkpoint

Jazmín 9:42PM
Haha n dnt call me back i know ur lies ur phone
broke u lost it or ur still at the checkpoint

MARCH 19, 2015

Jazmín 2:09AM
Thief

Alex 3:07AM
As a matter if fact I was with border patrol and
barely got out

Jazmín 3:12AM
May I sleep thank u gd bye

Alex 3:58AM
You always think wrong of me . . . call border
patrol and ask them. This lady is going to take
the ppl to Houston. Everything's ready for
tomorrow.

Flagrant disobedience, wrote Zuckerman in his mental note-
book, yet now Alex had successfully collected a more prof-
itable load of four people at the motel. Although Zuckerman
instinctively opposed authority, he understood Jazmín's fury.
He pictured her: *Latina, thirty-something, tight black clothes, 190
pounds, tattoos.* Slippery, charming Alex was probably in his
twenties. And really, thought Zuckerman, what were they,
both of them, but hard-working immigrants making their way
just like the Zuckermans in a new country?

MARCH 19, 2015

Jazmín 11:45AM
Answer ur freakin phone asshole

Jazmín 12:07PM
Look Alex I saw u in that hotel with ur whore so
dnt lie to me ur a thief and a frakin crackhead
either u do ur job or give me all my money back

Jazmín 12:27PM
Chingon

Jazmín 12:28PM
I need u2 get ur job done today

Jazmín 12:31PM
Ok dnt answer crackhead but u hurt my ppl time
to get even

Jazmín 1:08PM
Answer ur phone

Jazmín 4:17PM
U can run but u cant hide so answer

Alex 4:24PM
I really want to finish the job I beg you I'm ready
and hoping you let me work

Alex to Dustin 4:58PM
Please tell me you got one hit for me :-P

Dustin the dealer, noted Zuckerman. Like many of his own informants, Jazmín and Alex were probably both liars. Both spoke of "ppl" as a commodity like vegetables—which, in truth, they were.

Zuckerman liked and believed in truth, though he sometimes deviated from it himself. As an interviewer, he knew exactly when to sit back and nod, and when to press, either delicately or aggressively, but this was different. Now he was watching wildlife from a blind. He wondered if the phone was disposable and if so, rechargeable. Better hurry, he thought, because those agents might turn up any moment; they'd already been gone for half an hour.

He discovered that Jazmín and Alex were back on texting terms.

MARCH 20, 2015

Alex 12:05PM
Im calling you ma. This stupid lady is taking a bit
longer. Let me call you

Jazmín 12:33PM
Txt me when ur ready

Alex 1:27PM
This lady comes with more and more stories.
The guy with the license is here and we are
trying to open him a bank acout to get a credit
card . . . But if nothing happens within the next
2 hours I guess I'll move it to tomorrow to be on
the safe side

Jazmín 1:39PM
Nah its ok I cant b paying more hotel nights
work on getting my money back

Alex 1:40PM
No hold on let me try this first please mami

Jazmín 1:41PM
U have til 3
No more sweet talk no ma mami mamita I'm not
ur whore

Alex 1:41PM
Ok

Again, Zuckerman almost sympathized with Jazmín. Terms
of endearment never came easy to him, although women did.
And then they went.

"So many girlfriends," his mother once complained, while
also betraying a secret salacious glee. "How can you . . ." and

she hesitated, "*go* with all those girls, blacks, Orientals, Indians? Is it . . . different?"

"All cats," said Zuckerman, "are gray in the dark."

"James!" she exclaimed.

He shrugged.

"Well," huffed his mother, "if you can't say something nice, don't say anything at all."

"You asked."

After his father's death, Zuckerman decided to investigate his own family history, but a little digging quickly revealed that his forebears were not heroes. They weren't even Zuckermans. Apparently, his great-grandfather had taken the name, along with another man's papers, and possibly the contents of his pockets, during a hasty departure from Albania around 1900. The real ancestral name seemed to be Zog—far better suited to a family whose characteristic flavor, as Zuckerman well knew, was not sweet. But of course the Zucker bowls would never budge from his mother's shelves, not until he and his two sisters finally boxed them up, salted perhaps with a few Zog tears.

Zuckerman turned back to the cell phone.

MARCH 20, 2015

Dustin to Alex 2:28PM
Y'all had my ride to damn long

Alex 2:42PM
I don't have your ride and I know it's way to long and I truly apologize for it and of course will pay you. Let me ask do you have a valid drivers license and credit card to rent a car from enterprise?? Cuz I don't and I have ppl who need to go to Houston

Alex to Unknown 2:44PM
Hey bro do you have a valid driver license and credit card to rent a car??

Unknown 2:45PM
Whos this

Alex to Raúl 2:46PM
Hey bro do you have a valid driver license and credit card to rent a car??

Raúl 2:47PM
Who Da Fuk Is dis?

Alex to Dustin 2:55PM
How you doin? So, do you have a valid license and ATM card to rent a car?

Dustin 2:56PM
Yeah

Alex 2:57PM
Would you get me one for another 150$??
PLEASE! !!! you would save my ass from loosing my work

Dustin 3:01PM
I haven'T even got my car back yet but u want me to do something Getty my stuff and if I'm not still tripping bY then I got u

Alex to Briana 3:12PM
Can you rent me a car mami and I'll pay you 100$?

Briana 3:15PM
Why should I do that

Alex 3:16PM
I'll give you 100$ bucks

Briana 3:16PM
U are cucu

MARCH 21, 2015

Alex to Jazmín 1:11PM
I'll call you in a little bit

Jazmín 1:26PM
U better

Jazmín 2:30PM
U get the rental with ur moeny I dnt have time

Alex 2:34PM
I don't have any money you know that and now
I'm even more short then I was already. . . . The
rental we can get after we cross the next 2

Jazmín 2:36PM
Ur short cus ur a crackhead thats y but thats ur
problem not mine

Alex 2:42PM
When have you seen me smoking crack that
you keep calling me a crackhead??? I paid their
motel that's why and yes it's my problem, but
you said you were gonna help. I'll handle that by
getting a title loan or selling my car

Jazmín 2:44PM
My guys have seen u using drugs u even ofered
them n of course I belive them way more n I
want the rental now not after you cross kids
parents keep calling

Alex 2:50PM

So I'm a crackhead based on what you heard from somebody??? Cool. . . . We will be late to cross if we get the rental first

Jazmín 2:51PM

Just go cross crackhead N remember u told me u were on drugs

Alex 2:55PM

And I'm not a liar like you always accuse me of and I'm not a crackhead but don't matter

It was now 5:42 A.M. and a mockingbird ran through its repertoire nearby. Zuckerman was tired of standing, tired of waiting, and tired of all his companions. Bickering smugglers were just as tedious as any other distasteful coworkers, including stupid sleep-deprived Border Patrol agents. And Zuckerman was also tired of his miserable self.

"The problem is," he thought, "that everyone is wrong."

Jazmín and Alex were criminals, and Alex at least was a liar and apparently a crackhead. He summed them up in his mental notes: *scum*. But wasn't the U.S. the real villain, with its irrational drug and immigration laws, its unfairly distributed wealth, and its hordes of greedy drug-suckers? Yet other massively bad governments shouldn't be let off the hook. And now Zuckerman felt the horrible brain chaos building again. Why should he bother? This overpopulated world was doomed anyway, he thought. Coral reefs were perishing, icebergs vanishing. After Chernobyl, European mushrooms were unsafe to eat for ten thousand years. The longer he looked, the fewer absolutes he found. He would never write his book.

When his second ex-wife, Mona, had wanted a baby, Zuckerman nixed that: "Too many people in the world already!" Then came one of the rare moments when he read her thoughts as though they were spelled out in a bubble over her head: "Me too?"

Another memory intervened. He thought of Ana Claudia Villa Herrera, and then of the brown paper bag.

"No!" he said to both of them.

MARCH 21, 2015

Alex to Carmelita 3:17PM
Hey mami are you ready now?? This is Alex

> **Carmelita** 3:17PM
> U should pick someone else I'm having 2nd
> thoughts sorry I cant do it

Alex 3:19PM
Please don't let me down ma . . . I promise you
nothing bad will be done or happen and honestly
I don't have somebody else! You could even
come with me and I'll pay you plus its gonna be
fun on a road trip

> **Carmelita** 3:21PM
> Sorry
> Im so sorry I cant

Alex to Crystal 3:44PM
Come to the motel San Juan in. Are you gonna
leave me hanging too now? I won't get no more
work from that lady if we don't come through
now I got 2 more to cross tonite then all 8 go to
Houston together

> **Crystal** 4:21PM
> chilll bruh on the way homiee

Whoa, thought Zuckerman, *eight?* And who's Crystal, the underling's underling? Then he discovered that Alex wanted Crystal's car for the next border crossing. But how would they get eight passengers to Houston? They'd have to put the kids in the trunk.

MARCH 22, 2015

Crystal to Alex 12:27AM
como andas? wherre you at or what

Alex 12:27AM
Good barely getting to checkpoint

Crystal 12:28AM
oh ok becareful

Crystal 12:46AM
heyyy?

Crystal 12:47AM
call me or txt me back what happebnd?

Alex 12:58AM
You have weed in the car

Crystal 12:59AM
wheree? we dint have weed in the car.

Alex 1:01AM
Crumbs on the floor He said if that's all they find
im good cant hold me

Crystal 1:12AM
hows everything?

Alex 1:13AM
So far good stop calling thou I can't b on the
phone ma

Crystal 1:46AM

I want my car in an hour you better be here! and
I want my money this is the last time I do this
crap

A few weeks earlier, the ranch house had appeared to be abandoned. Harsh New Mexico weather had licked the paint from all the wood, and a shingle blew off the roof while Zuckerman stood there. Yet as he raised his hand to knock, the door swung open and a cowboy as weather-beaten as the house peered out. Before Zuckerman could explain his project, the man spread out his hands apologetically: "No English."

Zuckerman replied somewhat over-confidently that he spoke Spanish, but then a hoarse old voice called out from the back of the house.

"Eh! Rafael! *¿Quién es?*"

Zuckerman wondered if the speaker was a man or a woman.

"*No sé, patrona.*"

So, he thought, the boss is female.

"Come in, whoever you are," she yelled.

"*Pásale,*" said the cowboy, so Zuckerman followed him down a long hall hung with sepia photographs, mostly of people on horseback. The old lady was sitting at her kitchen table drinking bourbon from a coffee cup. She tilted a deeply corrugated face toward the stranger.

"Hey, Useless," she said. "What do you want?"

Zuckerman was actually silenced for a moment before launching into his usual spiel.

"A book about the border, eh?" she said when he was done. "Too many books in the world already, most of 'em bad. I thought you were one of those biology boys wanting to study my weeds or my horny toads." Before he could answer, she added sharply: "You might as well write a book about air."

"I—"

"Siddown," she said. "Since you're here you might as well stay, though I don't see what I can do for you, or you for me. Want some?" She pointed at the bourbon bottle.

"Thanks, not in the morning." Zuckerman regained some of his poise. "Can I ask you a few questions, then, Mrs.—"

"No Mrs. Long time ago, I got stuck with 'Sissy.'"

A most unlikely name for somebody who could sit slumped like a pile of old tires and still make men jump. Sissy's grandfather was the original homesteader, she said. "He came out here in 1879. He had some dogs and he had some hogs. Now everybody's gone but me and I couldn't keep it up without Rafael."

The cowboy retreated to a stool against the wall, his face so straight that it was hard tell how much he understood. Above his head, wandering water stains made the high kitchen ceiling look like an antique map.

"Long time ago, county sheriff brought him over 'cause the sheriff owed me a favor. Ha! Now Rafael and his family are just as legal as you." She flashed a row of false teeth. "*Are* you? Funny who is and who isn't. They all got amnesty in '86."

Discreetly touching his shirt pocket, Zuckerman asked about the changes Sissy must have seen along the border. She gave a laugh like a series of raven caws.

"When I was little," she said, "it wasn't even a string of bob wire."

She had raven eyes, too: "What's in your pocket? Can't you write, Tape Recorder Boy?"

She forced Zuckerman to turn it off and scrawl notes with a blunt pencil. Well, he thought, if she didn't care about word-for-word accuracy, then neither did he.

Harriet Bascom Steele—'Sissy' (b. 1920?) not called brder but la línea the Line—no fence, no nthg—nbdy cared—easy bk &

forth—not in P. Villa time tho—hung a man fr evry telephone pole—everybody poor poor poor—nvr enough rain—wild cattle—wild horses—screwworm—hoof & mouth—Depression—Okies—cooked a wolf—not even dogs wd eat it—polio—war—bro gone—prnts gone—hsbnd gone—nvr shd've mried bum—kids gone—drugs, bandits, smugglers—pistol—pillow—shotgun—closet—time to go.

Startled, Zuckerman looked up.

"Not you, Useless. Where's my cane? I want to show you something. Rafa!"

Rafael handed her a heavy wooden stick topped with a crudely carved rattlesnake's head.

Enough! Zuckerman returned to the present and bent his head over the cell phone.

MARCH 23, 2015

Alex to Vanessa 3:57PM
Just before he decided to punch me I told him dude get in the computer find out where yr cars impounded and how much so we can get it out. We were all bad ass I offered him another rock everything was good and then he gets his psycho moment out if the blue. What should I do???? Think bout it and if you find one good reason y, then I'll help him get his car out. BUT not for him I'll do that for you mami

Vanessa 3:59PM
I know

Love among the drugs, observed Zuckerman. But Alex was always wooing somebody, so maybe Vanessa simply owned a car. Or was it real, true, sucker-punch love? Why not, thought Zuckerman. The guy was a risk-taker. Likeable, too, in a crooked way, maybe even lovable. Zuckerman himself regarded love—a word and a condition that he preferred to avoid—as a series of sulfurous flashes that would scorch his fingers if he weren't careful, before they all burned out. Except for Mona? Yes, even Mona, Zuckerman told himself, but nevertheless he felt a needle pierce his heart.

On the cell phone it was March 23rd.

MARCH 23, 2015

Alex to Danny 5:34PM
Do you wanna make a hundred bucks by keeping 8 people for two days at your house?

Danny 5:56PM
If I could help I would man sorry

Alex 5:58PM
No that's fine bro I'll take them to a motel I would just prefer for someone to be watching them you know

Alex to Jazmín 7:28PM
Just crossed checkpoint :-)

Alex 8:22PM
Ok are we gonna call this even now and you talk to me?? Except that last ride to Denver everything went good and I thought we had found a solution together. So please answer me and let me know what's gonna happen from here, so I can start working on the next trip

Alex 10:37PM
I don't know if you are planning to pay me or not that's fine but can you please pay Lalo and

Crystal direct? They did their job and should be
laid please

Alex 10:37PM
Not laid I mean paid

Zuckerman wondered how many people were jammed into
the motel room now and if they were being fed. Simultane-
ously he noted that the time was 6:55 and the cell phone was
nearly dead. He suspected the Border Patrol agents were fill-
ing out their shift by napping somewhere.

MARCH 25, 2015

Crystal to Alex 12:26AM
Pagame!

Alex 12:34AM
Do you think I don't wanna pay you or if you
keep saying that, it will be faster??? Ay mamita
I told you I would pay you first. I begged her to
at least pay you and Lalo cuz y'all finished your
work. Please keep calling and keep bugging her,
worsed case threaten that you will report that
house to the migra or something.

Crystal 12:36AM
she dont answerr

Alex 12:37AM
I'm on it mami and I'm sorry but I have the
same issue. Text her that you are not gonna let
yourself be done like that and your mom wants
to go report to the migra or something

Alex to Vanessa 4:10PM

I'm back ma sorry I missed seeing you but my ppl werent in the motel no more . . . . . don't know what happened to them

Vanessa 4:11PM

Wtf?

Alex 4:12PM

So I came back. Maybe they got caught from the migra or if they left, but I think Jazmín stole em and I think I know where she put em. I was more happy and excited bout seeing you then anything else :(

Vanessa 4:12 PM

I know

If he ever did write the book, Zuckerman thought as he stood in the humid darkness, there might be a chapter called "Trees." From all his border travels, three particular trees stood out in his mind.

The first tree stood alone in the California desert, wild, scraggly, and unwatered, yet much taller than Zuckerman himself. It was definitely the biggest marijuana plant he'd ever seen. The second tree was an urban sapling barely surviving in front of the Federal Courthouse in Phoenix. During an immigration demonstration, a group of women knelt on the sidewalk and prayed and wept before an image of the Virgin of Guadalupe that dangled from one of the stunted branches. Cat food. Zuckerman backed away.

He squashed the thought, suffocated it: *Don't let it spook you. You just have to get through this one night, March 30, that's all.* And he looked down at the phone and saw that now the texters were catching up to him. They had reached March 26th.

MARCH 26, 2015

Alex to Crystal 3:22PM
I now found out why she don't answer me and
since you and Lourdes are kind of responsible
you keep trying to call her cuz she doesn't
answer me. I can't pay no one until she answers.
You know where she lives just like I do… we
need to get ahold of her to get paid.

Crystal 3:25PM
me and Lourdes? how are we responsible?

Alex 3:27PM
When y'all talked crap bout me to her, that's y
she didn't answer me. Ive talked to a chivo of
hers he told me that some girls called her bout me

Crystal 3:37PM
we dint talk crap about you we gave facts, now I
aint supose to look for her you are

Alex 3:39PM
Well you shouldve thought that the first time
when y'all did call her, now that y'all screwed it
up for everybody you wanna put it back on me?

Crystal 3:41PM
thanks to us nah thanks to you. your the fkg
dumbass that fkd it up for evryone rather have
that crack then have clients, get your head right

Crystal 4:00PM
try to get some gas money and well go look for
this lady see wassup

Alex 4:01PM
I don't have gas money you know where it's at,
go ahead

Sissy had led him to the third tree, which was a common hackberry that grew beside a garbage dump and staging area for smugglers, just north of the international line. Sissy waved her rattlesnake cane at the tree, where every thorn seemed to be festooned with rags, but she explained, "Those are women's panties. We call this the rape tree."

"How do I know that's true?" objected Zuckerman. "Maybe right-wingers made it to fool politicians. And journalists."

"Ha!" Sissy crowed. "Don't really matter, they oughta be dead. Love to kill 'em myself. They say the girls take pills before they start the trip," she added, hobbling back toward her filthy pickup.

"Wait a minute," said Zuckerman. "What's that?"

He pointed to a scruffy little structure that stood beneath the tree. A bunch of sun-bleached fake flowers bristled over its gaping doorway and in the shadows behind a pool of cold candle grease he caught a glimpse of a small white figure in a flowing robe, holding a scythe. Was this some sort of depraved dollhouse?

"Ha," Sissy said again. "It's Santa Muerte, Dumbo. Dontcha know Saint Death when you see 'er?"

Now Zuckerman perceived the tiny skull beneath the headdress, and the skeletal fingers that clutched the scythe.

"La Flaquita. Skinny Lady. Made-up saint of death, though I guess most saints are made-up when you get right down to it. But Santa Muerte likes night, crime, hell, drugs, bones, smugglers, murderers, cops, waitresses, whores, and corpses. And borders. You two should get acquainted."

Zuckerman found himself absolutely struck dumb all the

way back to the pickup, which Sissy gunned across the wash-board road, rattling his teeth.

"Time to go," she yelled over the rumble.

"Okay," yelled Zuckerman.

"Not you, Pea Brain. Me. I'm ready."

She hit the brakes, and flesh-colored dust swirled through the truck. "I wake up every morning and think, 'Damn, I'm still alive.'"

Zuckerman coughed and choked.

Then she raised the cane again, nearly whacking his nose, and pointed out the passenger window. "Rafa's already dug my grave."

Again, Zuckerman was speechless.

"Over there next to that big old boulder, just the way I want it. See it? He made it nice and deep. My kids never do anything right."

As they approached the house Sissy said, for no particular reason: "Used to have an old cowboy who didn't even know what side of the Line he was born on. Nor exactly when, either. His mama told him under a shade tree on a ranchito, coulda been New Mexico, coulda been Chihuahua, but she was long gone. Fulgencio . . . missing two fingers, and he's long gone too. Course *he* never had any kind of paper at all."

To Zuckerman's dismay, just as he tried to make his getaway Rafael turned up carrying a paper bag and asked permission to show him something. Why the hell, thought Zuckerman impatiently, would I want to see some cowboy's lunch?

On the phone it was still March 26.

MARCH 26, 2015

Alex to Dustin 7:26PM

If I get 8 stolen ppl, do you have a place to keep

them and do you know how to get money out of
them? Call me

Alex to Dustin 10:40PM
You wanna go to Houston with 2 kids
n 6 men? I'll pay 400 a head

Dustin 10:45PM
Idk
Where they at

Alex 10:49PM
McAllen
Pretty smooth and easy bro
$$$$$$$$$$$$$$

Dustin 10:52PM
Ok

Zuckerman absorbed this. So—the boys were going into business for themselves, maybe not for the first time. They played a wild game: high stakes, no rules. But, he thought, *what happened to those eight captives?*

Suddenly, the mesquites seemed oddly quiet. After that rattle of gunfire an hour ago, he'd heard nothing but birdsong, and now he heard nothing at all. The sun was high enough to illuminate most shadows, but was something—or someone—out there? Idiot, he scolded himself, don't be so corny. Maybe those agents were finally coming back and the wildlife knew first.

Across the clearing, the mesquite branches grew low and thick and became almost opaque. But there in the midst of them, about two feet off the ground, he saw two greenish golden eyes, and the eyes saw him.

"Optical illusion," Zuckerman told himself, and quickly looked down at the phone, where he saw that time had passed. It was now March 29th.

MARCH 29, 2015

Dustin to Alex 7:15PM
U want to cross some people?

Alex 7:16PM
How many?

Dustin 7:16PM
U can talk to my friend
He said they put them in the trunk its up to u if u
want to do it

Dustin 8:13PM
Yes r no r u got to think about it

Zuckerman drew a deep breath and tried to stop a sudden attack of memories.

Rafael's brown paper bag was heavy, as though it contained a large piece of fruit. Impatiently Zuckerman looked inside, and gasped.

It was not a grapefruit. It stared back at him with deep vacant eye sockets, yet a few curly hairs still clung to the scalp and the brows. Half head, half skull, once it had belonged a man about his own age.

"Where did you get this?"

Rafael said he had found it yesterday in a distant pasture.

"You need to call the police. You should've left it there." He thought of Ana Claudia Villa Herrera's fingers scattered like dice. "What about the rest of the bones?"

Rafael shook his head. "*Nada*," he said. "I looked for an hour."

"No!"

"*Sí.*"

"How can that be?"

As straight-faced as ever, Rafael raised his own eyes and gave Zuckerman a look.

"Here, take it," said Zuckerman, beginning to understand and not liking it. This severed head was going to bother him. It looked horribly familiar. "Why didn't you just leave it there? It could be dangerous."

"It's a human being," Rafael said.

No. No! Quickly Zuckerman looked down at the phone.

MARCH 29, 2015

Alex 8:29PM
Tell him walking I could take 5 at a time and I'll charge him only 1800 a head. Pick up here and deliver in Houston

Dustin 8:31PM
They dont want to walk

Alex 8:33PM
Ok yeah worse case I'll take them through the line

Dustin 8:34PM
So if not u will still do it in the trunk

Alex 8:35PM
Not in the trunk but if poss I'll get them fake papers and take them through the line otherwise walk em

Another unwelcome memory attacked Zuckerman. A few miles north of the border, not far from Sissy's ranch, the Sons of Liberty had set up camp. By the time Zuckerman arrived, they had raised a big American flag inside a circle of eight or ten RVs that had seen better days. Like wasps, vigilantes buzzed around this headquarters. The Sons, who included quite a few stout Daughters, had mounted a "citizen surveillance" campaign called "Secure the Boot Heel of New Mexico." All of them were white and nobody was younger than fifty. Everyone was packing a gun, including the grannies. They were watching for migrants and smugglers; the Border Patrol was watching them, as well as the migrants and smugglers; and various other observers were watching the whole scene.

As he loitered curiously on the outskirts of the camp, Zuckerman noticed a young Hispanic man seated in a folding lawn chair and reading a large book.

"Law?" asked Zuckerman, touching the recorder in his pocket.

The young man nodded. He and several other law students had formed a team to monitor the Sons of Liberty.

"But so far," said the student, "almost nothing has happened."

Zuckerman laughed. "A losers' club?" he suggested.

"Why do we have borders?" asked the young man earnestly. "What if there were no borders at all?"

Dreamer, thought Zuckerman.

MARCH 29, 2015

Dustin 8:36PM
Lt me know how its goin
Watch ur back bro Jaz is pissd

Alex 8:37PM
OK but my phone will be off if I jump outa the car
to walk people ;-)

Dustin 8:38PM
How long u gone b

Alex 8:40PM
Never know

Dustin 8:43PM
I got some killer rock :-P

Alex 8:44PM
10/4
I'll be back before morning :)

Alex 10:01PM
So far so good

The mesquite thickets remained loudly silent, and finally Zuckerman forced himself to look again. The green-gold eyes were still gazing at him—large unblinking eyes, slightly slanted and set about two inches apart. Zuckerman yelled and banged on the Border Patrol logo on the side panel of the Suburban. Man or beast, that should do it, he thought. Meanwhile the cell phone offered a refuge, where he saw that the story on the little screen had reached the early hours of March 30, today, just a few hours ago.

MARCH 30, 2015

Dustin 12:30AM
Wasup

Dustin 12:33AM
Bro

Dustin 12:33AM
R u ok

Dustin 12:37AM
Txt me

???

Question marks. That was the end, the place where he'd first turned on the phone and begun to read the texts in the dark. Now he would never know what happened. And he had no excuse to stall anymore: if they were still staring at him, he must deal with those eyes. But then some belated texts began to arrive, bing after bing. He saw that they were also dated March 30, 2015. Today.

Jazmín to Alex 12:58AM

U stole my ppl u hurt my ppl time to get even

Alex to Dustin 12:59AM

Bfkkkkkkk

Jazmín 1:09AM

Just u keep in mind asshole crackhead

Dustin to Alex 1:09 AM

????????????

Jazmín 1:09AM

that karma is a real bitch

Zuckerman waited breathlessly, but there seemed to be nothing more. He shoved the phone into his pocket and moved toward the low mesquites, where the eyes continued to shine. As he got closer, he noted for future reference that mesquite leaves were composed of innumerable tiny green leaflets, and that mesquite thorns looked a lot like hypodermic needles. Then the whole picture leaped into focus, and he saw that the eyes belonged to a coyote.

"Get away!" he shouted, waving his arms.

The coyote floated into the bushes, unabashed.

Zuckerman found himself on all fours in the mud with his mouth full of slime, acid, vomit, and bile. He spat out as much as he could.

"You're getting soft!" he yelled at himself. "Old and soft!"

Then he leaned against the Suburban and tried to control his ragged breathing and the unusual beating of his heart. Un-Zuckermanlike fantasies careened through his brain. Maybe the Dreamer was right after all. Suddenly, Zuckerman had a vision of a great infernal wall of wall-enthusiasts, all doomed to stand along the border shoulder to shoulder throughout eternity, each body wrapped in a shiny space blanket. He imagined vending machines selling cheap passes like train tickets at all border crossings. He imagined the Border Patrol repositioned as a travel and job placement agency.

Dreamer yourself, he thought.

The higher the sun rose, the shorter Zuckerman's shadow grew. Seven o'clock went by, then 7:30. At long last he heard stumbles and curses in the bushes, and the five agents reappeared, muddy, bleeding, and disconsolate, but Zuckerman was sincerely glad to see them.

"Hey, Jim."

"Nothing?"

"Naw. Let's go home."

"Well, no," Zuckerman said. "I'm afraid not." Apologetically, he pointed toward the mesquite thicket. "Look over there."

He never did see his way in. Instead, as he stood there fingering the cell phone in his pocket, he distinctly heard a croak in his ear.

"If it was a snake, Useless, you'd be bit."

He choked. Auditory hallucinations! Sleep deprivation, maybe? He covered his ears but Sissy's harsh voice still came through, worse than cat food.

"You're looking right at it!"

Zuckerman felt a sickening whack of vertigo, as though she'd dangled him by his heels for an instant before she dropped him on his face. And yet he knew he'd never moved. Did other women consider him useless too? Sudden pain wrenched the left side of his chest.

"I've been shot!" he thought, clutching at his heart, but his shirt was dry. Then he was terrified that he would weep out loud but somehow managed to gulp down his sadness. Just for an instant Zuckerman remembered the crumbling red hole that Rafael had dug in the sand, and he wondered crazily if it still lay empty.

"*Ay, qué bonita,* pretty baby, *huesuda,* skeleton girl!" Now the voice was half cackle, half croon. "Throw 'er a bone, boy! Blow 'er some smoke. She likes *la droga* and she *loves* tequila 'cause she's an alcoholic. Yes, yes, always thirsty, always hungry, and has she ever gotta sweet tooth, our lady of black and white, our mother of justice!"

Oh no. He'd have to find a therapist. He'd certainly have to find a therapist.

But yes. There it was. His story.

Protector of the desperate and the weak, Santa Muerte raised her scythe above a restless crowd. Appalled, Zuckerman beheld faces that he recognized and some that he didn't, but he knew he'd probably met them all along the border, and far off to the side, looking very short and sad, he also saw himself.

Meanwhile, the Border Patrol agents had tramped across the clearing. They discovered the dark shape lying on the ground, and one by one they turned to stare at him.

"I haven't touched a thing," called Captain Death.

The Witch of the Stacks

Long, long ago, almost before computers, an old woman wandered through the library of a great American university. She was a short old woman with big feet that shuffled loudly down the dim linoleum aisles, and all the while she muttered incomprehensible syllables, she sniffed, she tapped her way along.

Choosing a book, she fell quiet. But not two seconds later she was startled—a sound? a draft?—and raised a suspicious face surrounded by loops and strings of gray hair. Beneath her thorny chin, her sweaters hung in more loops, and below them her skirts dangled unevenly. She was also wearing baggy trousers that once perhaps had belonged to a small man. Quickly she slapped the book shut, tucked it into a skinny armpit, and escaped with her prize.

She had a carrel at the top of the library but she rarely sat there long. Her little cell was full of books checked out on extended loan, pencil stubs, candy wrappers, and slips of paper inscribed with spiky German handwriting, then gathered in bunches, secured with straight pins, and heaped on the table. Gradually the sides of the heap had perfectly achieved the angle of repose.

Soon afterward, a new graduate student sat at work in the room reserved for doctoral candidates in the highly prestigious Literature and Thought program, and behind his back an argument broke out in hisses. He tried to concentrate on the Anglo-Saxon lament he was deciphering, but when the voices rose he turned around, just as an old woman darted off and slammed the door behind her. A second-year student, flushed and chagrined, spread out his papers on one of the scarred tables nearby.

Weeks later, the new graduate student observed the same

old woman mumbling to herself in the card catalogue, and once when he entered the coffee room, there she was, buttonholing an bald, embarrassed scholar. As bitter black fluid trickled into his paper cup, the student overheard:

"Of course Panofsky's theory—"

"Absolutely ridiculous!" she snapped.

Autumn advanced. First orange, then brown leaves drifted down upon the cobblestones in front of the library; soon ice made them dangerous. The graduate student tiptoed and skidded across the rocks, his endurance tested in every way. His room was frigid, the food bad, and his fiancée, who was enrolled in a lesser program in a lesser university, remote. He doubted his vocation for this life. And then in "The Medieval Lyric" his professor assigned him an arbitrary essay topic.

"Baudri de Bourgeuil?" The young man, a devotee of contemporary poetry and a published poet himself, stared in dismay. But two medieval courses were required for the degree.

"Minor eleventh-century French poet. He's in the Patrologia."

"Patrologia?"

"The writings of the Fathers of the Church."

A curious little smile puckered the professor's distinguished features.

Like masonry, the Patrologia lined a long library aisle, and there Baudri de Bourgeuil was indeed entombed. But he wrote exclusively in Latin and had failed for over eight hundred years to attract English translators. The new student feared that his Latin was too poor for the task. Perhaps he could scrape by with French? Then he discovered that every publication relating to Baudri in Latin, English, French, German, or Italian had been borrowed on extended loan by the same person.

"Klara Kaspar," said the librarian. "Doktor Frau Doktor Kaspar."

"Can't I just call them back in?"

"According to the rules you can, but she won't give them up. Try to persuade her to lend them to you for a few hours."

He peered through the window of her carrel and identified the books that he needed in a tall stack on the floor. Covertly he rattled the door but it was locked. He scoured the library for Klara Kaspar.

"Her!" exclaimed a fourth-year student. "Good luck."

"Who is she?"

"Widow of Wolfgang Kaspar, the great medievalist. They came to escape the Nazis, and after he died the university gave her a carrel and special lifetime privileges. Supposedly she's been working on the same book for forty years."

"What does she look like?"

"You must have seen her. They call her the Witch of the Stacks."

"Ah!"

His anger mounted. After the Rhodes and the other scholarships, the prizes, the precocious publications, the glory, why must he play this game? At last he caught her as she sidled up to her carrel. He managed to blurt out his request, and to his astonishment she handed over the books almost meekly.

"But," she called after him, "I need them tonight. I will meet you here at five o'clock."

"Fine!"

Photocopies would solve his problem. Then she could keep the damned books, which he noted she'd first checked out in 1953. By the time she reappeared at five on the dot, he'd squeezed the meaning out of several little poems and concocted a respectable paper. It even included a graceful English translation of some lines composed in Brittany, where the homesick poet yearned for the sweet roses of Bourgeuil. Baudri's Latin proved to be surprisingly simple.

"Thank you."

She grasped the books. "Professor McCannon is your teacher?"

"Yes."

"A brilliant scholar."

"Yes." Suddenly the student realized that his professor had purposely set up this obstacle course—Klara Kaspar, Latin doggerel, and all. It was a test. Hence his smirk. Well, well. With a flash of malice he continued: "And yet McCannon's number isn't extraordinarily high."

"Number?"

"Yes, haven't you heard about the number system?"

"No."

"Well," he said, "in this country, everyone is assigned a number, according to his, or her . . . quality. You didn't know?"

She shook her head. He noticed that behind thick, flawed lenses her eyes were the clearest and purest of blues. Once she must have been a blonde.

"You must be very pleased with *your* number, young man," she said.

"Yes, I—" He felt an odd icy pang. "I must say that I am," he added lamely.

Subsequently, he always avoided her, even sometimes ducking down a different library aisle. He took his doctorate and his honors and departed for his own brilliant career.

After a couple of decades he returned on sabbatical, a full professor elsewhere and writing a book that wandered, somehow. Year after year went by and he couldn't seem to finish it. It fluttered away like a black butterfly just ahead of his net, and meanwhile smaller and smaller magazines rejected his poems. Secret doubts gnawed him. He hadn't won any prizes for quite a long time, and yet somehow his wife had just become a dean. One day as he climbed toward the top of the library he remembered Klara Kaspar.

The carrel was scrupulously neat. A laptop computer, a white tablet, and two sharp pencils lay in exact alignment, while behind them marched a row of books with mathematical titles. Unconsciously, he crushed the paper in his hand.

So, he thought, Baudri de Bourgeuil had returned to the stacks at last, shoulder to shoulder in the half-light with the famous, the lesser known, and the obscure.

After a moment another thought struck him: there must be a computer monitor on this floor. He blundered about, running into several dead ends before he finally found a monitor near a door that stood open to the landing served by both the stairs and the elevator.

He tapped a few keys before he recalled that his own laptop was in his bag. But here, password- and fumble-free, was instant access to the big data banks, the magical modern Patrologia. Once long ago he'd encountered his Old English professor deep in the stacks and casually suggested how convenient it would be to have a card catalogue on every floor. The old man seemed ready to chop him up with a *seax* at the very suggestion. "Quite impossible!" he snapped. Yet here it was.

Baudri (also Baudry, Balderic, Balderico, Baldricus, and Baldwin) lay at his fingertips: abbot of Bourgeuil in the Loire Valley and, after the usual political machinations, archbishop of Dol-en-Bretagne. But then his career took a dive, for he stopped writing and was demoted to plain bishop, dying in late old age. "Wrote a number of Latin poems of very indifferent quality," sniffed the *Encyclopaedia Britannica*.

And yet that's unfair, thought the middle-aged scholar. As an enthusiastic scribbler of verse letters, particularly to boys, nuns, and ladies, surely Baudri had earned a modest place in literature, if only for his remarkable letter that described the Bayeux Tapestry when it was new.

Then he felt a disturbance in the air. Instead of the familiar aroma of library—paper, ink, glue, dust, floor wax, and a delicate touch of must—he smelled food, cheap food hot off a steam table. Food in the library? No, no, no! What about spills and vermin? Deep in his wallet he still cherished his old reader's ticket from the Bodleian Library, where he had signed a promise to obey all rules, not to mark, deface, or injure anything, and above all "not to bring into the Library or kindle therein any fire or flame."

The smell grew stronger. Cabbage and soy sauce, he thought, stepping indignantly into the lobby, where he found an overweight young man hunched on a bench, gobbling something brown and stringy from a Styrofoam clamshell. He threw the professor a truculent look ("Don't you dare interrupt my lunch!") and the older man silently returned to his computer.

After few more taps on the keyboard, he discovered that Baudri had found new followers in the past thirty or forty years. He experienced a mild but genuine pleasure, as though an unpromising student had excelled in later life. "Bravo, Baudri!" he said under his breath and read on. Feminists and gay-literature specialists had discovered the dethroned archbishop, along with Baudri's irony, double entendres, double lives, and secret meanings. Heloise . . . Abelard . . . Patrologia . . . patriarchy. Nuns were undercover radicals who said the opposite of what they meant. And clearly, when Baudri wrote of roses, he referred to not to flowers but to the cheeks of the boys he loved.

"Yes, perhaps," mused the man at the computer. Almost any meaning, he recalled, could flavor a layer of the great cake of Christian allegory.

To glimpse the possible in the unknown. Or the possible in the unknowable. That's what it's all about, he thought, isn't it? Thinking. Games of the mind. Ideas: just as real, just as solidly kickable, as boulders. He looked down at his hands on the keyboard and pictured green leaves budding from his fingertips, a very odd but delightful sensation. He hadn't felt such a feathery lift for a long, long time.

Giggles.

He gave a start. People were laughing at him, weren't they?

He heard more giggles, followed by a few unintelligible words in a woman's voice. Ah, he thought with relief, of course, she's out in the lobby. A man's voice replied in the same language, louder. The scholar listened carefully but did not understand a single word, so it couldn't be one of his own four or five languages. As the high and low voices continued quietly to converse, he shook off the interruption and turned back to the screen. Just before the giggles, he thought he'd glimpsed a familiar name.

Yes, there it was, in a footnote to an essay on gay love letters of the Middle Ages: *McCannon*. Swiftly he located McCannon's article, published in a top journal, likely printed in elegant type on fancy paper. In those days the pages crackled in a stately way when you turned them, yet here was McCannon now, spread out in two dimensions on the screen like an X-ray.

The voices in the lobby had risen. They were speaking whatever language it was in normal tones, laughing and flirting. A spurt of pop music interrupted them—probably a ringtone from someone's phone, because it abruptly ceased, followed by even louder gabble. "Now, now," the older man scolded himself, "they're just kids. Never mind." The library at his university was quieter than this, but mainly because at any given time most of its users were draped over the furniture, fast asleep. Possibly this helped to explain a recent outbreak of bed bugs among the books.

The visiting scholar forced his attention back to the article, which was dated several years after he'd received his own A+ in "The Medieval Lyric." Skimming the lengthy title and even longer subtitle, he caught Baudri's name as well as "Loire Poets," "Courtly Love," and "Roman de la Rose." Immersed as he personally was in modern and contemporary poetry, of course he'd never run across his old professor's work. He began to read.

Thumps, squeals, and peals of laughter distracted him. Now he heard roughhousing or perhaps erotic activity on the other side of the wall. He sighed and got up again, just to check, and there in a row on the bench he discovered a tall youth crowned with blue-black curls, flanked by two young women in pretty hijabs that showed a bit of their own glossy dark hair. They had been speaking Arabic, he guessed, but at the sight of him they stopped dead, mouths open. Six black eyes stared, unsmiling.

"Oh, excuse me," he murmured politely, and turned away. That should be enough of a hint, he thought.

He hadn't read anything remotely like this article for decades, so why did the text seem familiar? Maybe it awakened memories of McCannon's interminable lectures, even though he assumed he'd forgotten them. He plowed along diligently, still wondering, until he came to the poem.

Baudri's roses. His translation.

He was certain. He'd translated it as he waited outside Klara Kaspar's carrel that autumn afternoon. It was an accurate but rather loose translation because he'd let the English words have their heads in the end. How much of the rest of his essay had McCannon stolen? His student typescript was long gone; he would never know.

Faint but clear, youthful mimicry pierced the wall: "Oh, excuse me!" More giggles. They *were* laughing at him. He leaped through the doorway.

"Quiet! Shut up! Get out of here!"

Still furious, he watched them clatter down the stairs. Then he turned his back and plunged into the stacks. He wandered, aimless and remorseful, until he came a place where rows of bookshelves were clamped together to save space. At the touch of a button they would grind apart, when not malfunctioning, but he always felt uneasy around so-called compact shelving. It was the perfect place for an academic murder—or execution.

Klara Kaspar was long gone and McCannon too; he'd seen the obituary. And as for Baudri de Bourgeuil . . .

"Go back and copy that poem, you damned fool," he urged himself. "Do you want to lose it again?"

Then something hit him like a punch in the face. He stopped dead in the twilight with tears scalding his eyes, for instead of old glue and musty paper, suddenly he smelled the heady fragrance of a live red rose.

Shoot

"Don't blame the pigs." That's what Jack always said, afterward.

True enough. Those pigs never murdered anything, much less a whole artistic genre. Or a genre, anyway.

And yet mathematics will show that any great catastrophe may be traced back to a lone, faraway blip. One blip leads unpredictably to another and another. Blackboards chalked from top to bottom with weird symbols and numbers definitely prove that if a butterfly flaps her wings in Xanadu, that one little flutter could eventually cause a tornado in Timbuktu. This is called chaos theory.

Neither the butterfly nor the pigs deliberately set out to make trouble. Or, for that matter, to cause change. Nor did Jack, who was just a scrawny ranch kid in those days, nor his stone-faced old dad, Wendell the rancher, because chaos is chaotic, not deliberate. The Hollywood actors were pretty much innocent too, especially since the only actor who played a role in the actual debacle was a dummy. Even so, sooner or later the finger of cosmic blame always points at human beings, who do deliberately make trouble, and probably there's math to prove that too. Here there were two red-handed agents of disaster: the movie director and, even guiltier, the scriptwriter. You might say it was a real-life example of the good, the bad, and the ugly.

Getting back to the pigs, of course they weren't really pigs. That's just their common name. Actually, they were peccaries or javelinas, native Southwestern animals that look rather like wild boars but even more like fifty-pound scrub brushes with big sharp teeth. They're not even in the pig family. They tiptoe around on tiny hoofs and scavenge roots, bugs, carrion, cactus, and putrid garbage, which is exactly what they smell like, only worse. They ooze a foul musk that smells like Chanel Coco Mademoiselle perfume . . . to other javelinas.

The year was 1962 and the place was Cochise County, Arizona, where once upon a time a Western movie was being filmed. Named for the Apache hero (played by Jeff Chandler, born in Brooklyn as Ira Grossel) of the movie *Broken Arrow*, Cochise County fills the bottom right-hand corner of the state, teetering on the edge of both New and Old Mexico. And of course the rather dubious town of Tombstone still stands in Cochise County.

But this was a different movie. The cast did not include John Wayne or Clint Eastwood. According to the script, which owed quite a bit to *Oklahoma,* a bandido with a mustachio (born in Brooklyn as Carmine Orrico but rechristened Johnny Saxon when he moved to Hollywood) falls for a rancher's daughter (played by a blonde starlet named Nina Shipton). His love is doomed. The girl's rancher father (George Montgomery) throws the boyfriend off the ranch. Then in a tragic finale only possible in an L.A. scriptwriter's imagination, the bandido is attacked and devoured by a raging horde of bloodthirsty javelinas.

That's where the writer took a shameless plunge into crime. There's plenty of proof that javelinas are biters—dog biters, prickly-pear biters, petunia biters, and, yes, man biters. But there's not one scrap of evidence that they're either man killers or man eaters. They much prefer garbage.

The nonfictional ranchers, Wendell and Jack, had worked for this director before, providing dogs, horses, and wrangling skills when he'd visited Cochise County to shoot such films as *The Wetback Hound Dog* and *The Cactus Killer.* The money was good, and Westerns were glamorous. But now the director asked for twenty large, live, homicidal javelinas.

Wendell voiced no opposition but thought it over carefully,

and then he applied to the Arizona Department of Game and Fish for a wildlife-handling permit. Somewhat to his surprise the Game and Fish approved the plan as long as no javelinas were injured and all returned to their own natural habitat after their movie careers were over. So, permit in hand, Jack and Wendell set out to catch wild pigs for the Hollywood director. But javelinas don't really have necks, and crosswise they're flat, not round like pigs and cows. Genuine wild boars do have some bristles, but javelinas are as prickly as porcupines, and they totally lack horns and tusks. There's just not much to get ahold of.

"Roping a javelina," Jack always used to say, "is like roping a mean old hairy flounder."

Days went by, but they managed to chase down only two of the beasts. Of course their ranch country was very rough and brushy, which didn't help. So finally they unleashed their hunting dogs, who succeeded in bringing javelinas to bay like mountain lions. Still, it cost father, son, horses, and dogs several weeks of hard work to round up twenty head.

They corralled these javelinas in a large pen and fed them well on corn and mescal plants washed down with lots of fresh water. Jack and Wendell also built the hogs a large plywood box with a sliding door where the future movie stars liked to shelter, especially at night. They seemed to feel safe when they were holed up inside the box, which was lined with straw, and over time they gradually settled down to life in the pen with regular meals and a snug hideout.

Then they got their cue. Time to shoot the big scene! So Wendell and Jack herded the javelinas into a livestock trailer and trucked them and their box to the movie location, thinking that the familiar box would make the animals feel less stressed during the trip and the shoot. The place was no Monument Valley, but it was picturesque. The ranchers built another pigpen on the hillside where the director planned to set the scene, and they installed the box of javelinas at the top of the hill. The fenced area included several high rocky bluffs on either side of a clear pathway or natural chute, which ran down the slope.

The director explained his vision. "Now, Wendell, we want those javelinas to come busting down the hill in a cluster."

"Cluster?"

"Yes. And then bang! They attack this dummy at the bottom of the hill."

The life-size dummy somewhat resembled the star of the show, Johnny Saxon (a.k.a. Carmine Orrico). It even had a mustache.

"They're furious. Crazed. Frothing at the mouth." To demonstrate, the director grimaced and waved his hands wildly. "In a frenzy, they rip his body to shreds with their tusks!"

This was the scenario the scriptwriter had dreamed up. To capture the horrific action from above, the director planned to station several camera operators atop the rock outcrops on the hillside. But knowing something about javelinas, Wendell studied the situation carefully and shook his head.

"Well, now," he said. "I'm not so sure they'll bunch up and run downhill."

That was a long speech for Wendell. At the moment, of course, all the javelinas were still hiding in the box.

Wendell slightly adjusted his cowboy hat, a signal of strong feeling. "What if they run up into the rocks instead?" he asked.

The director roared with laughter.

"What?" he scoffed. "Of course they'll run straight down the hill! I never saw a pig that could climb a rock."

Even though the director seemed to be an animal expert,

Wendell adjusted his hat again and raised another objection. "They might jump the fence at the bottom and run away, " he said. "If they get that far."

"Okay," said the director. "Then we'll hold up a big tarp on the other side of the dummy to block 'em."

Wendell shrugged and jammed his hat straight. The movie people ran up and down and around in circles setting things up, and pretty soon he found himself holding one edge of the tarp at the bottom of the hill. Young Jack was given the job of running the javelinas out of their box, even though they huddled there in a bristly pile and persistently refused to move.

"Make 'em run!" yelled the director.

Jack inched a little farther into the box and waved his arms. He didn't like to get too close because the pigs were clicking their teeth (not wild-boar tusks, but plenty sharp) and growling at him, and the scareder they got, the more they stank.

"Hoo!" he yelled. "Git!"

But they still refused to budge.

The director turned to Wendell. "Huh! What makes them run in the wild?"

Wendell thought for a moment. "Gunfire?" he suggested.

So somebody found a .38 caliber pistol lying around the set and loaded it with blanks, and the director gave Jack his orders: "Wait for me to shout 'Action!' If you can't stir 'em up, fire, and start the stampede."

"Yessir."

Jack grasped the pistol. The twenty confused javelinas were still hiding in their box.

"But don't shoot the pistol into the air because I don't want any smoke in this scene," warned the director.

"Okay," said Jack. "If I have to shoot it, I'll point it to the ground."

Just before filming finally started, a prop man came walking up to the box where Jack was warily keeping his distance from the hostile javelinas. He had armed himself with a sheet of plywood to use as a shield and a pusher.

"I know what'll really make those hogs run," the man said in a confidential tone.

"What's that?" asked Jack.

"Well," the prop man said, "we'll sprinkle them with a little 'high life.' That won't hurt them, just burn their hides a little, and they'll run like hell!"

"What's high life?" said Jack.

"Aw, it's just a chemical that evaporates real fast," said the prop man.

Presto! He produced a brown glass bottle, and without further ado he began to sprinkle high life on the javelinas' backs. Quite a lot of the liquid also spilled on the straw underfoot as well as on Jack. To him, high life smelled like a gas leak or rotten eggs . . . just a little better than javelinas. It did seem to make his skin burn. Later he learned that the real name of the stuff was carbon disulfide, or CS_2 and it was a powerful solvent used to make rayon and also as an insecticide.

By this time it was high noon and an audience had gathered. Besides the movie crew members, curious local people, and random passers-by, a busload of drama students had arrived from the University of Arizona in Tucson to observe how a movie was made, and so, what with the drama teachers and the bus driver, it added up to a pretty good crowd.

Stinging slightly, Jack got into position inside the box, where he held the plywood shield in his left hand and the pistol in his right.

"Action!" hollered the director.

But even though they were drenched with high life, the javelinas refused to move. Jack slid the door as wide open as it would go and gave the pigs a slight shove. They grumbled and twitched but held tight.

"Fire!"

So Jack aimed the barrel of the pistol at the ground because the director didn't want to see any gunsmoke, and he squeezed the trigger. But instead of a gunshot, the next thing he heard was an earsplitting boom.

Carbon disulfide is also highly flammable. When the pistol sparked, the soaked straw burst into flames and the wooden box exploded. Jack found himself flying backward out of the pen while the javelinas lit out in the opposite direction. Everybody and everything in the immediate area was smoking. Meanwhile the drama students clapped and cheered. As far as they could tell, it was all part of the movie.

Totally ignoring the dummy, the inflamed animals raced straight up the rocks that the director swore they'd never climb, toppled the tripods, and chased off the cameramen. Top speed for a normal javelina is maybe twenty to thirty miles an hour, but a burning one runs quicker. Those movie fellows abandoned their cameras and squealed and hollered as they bailed off boulders and hurtled over fences in a mad dash to get away from the angry javelinas.

Meanwhile Jack gathered himself up from the ground, choking and coughing. First he aimed a few whacks at his smoldering shirt and Levi's. Then he saw that the pig house was all blown to pieces and on fire, and most of the javelinas were steaming off in the distance like so many small-gauge locomotives. But two of them were still hunched in the flames and wreckage, too stunned and confused to escape. Jack jumped into the ruins of the box, grabbed one javelina by the prickly hind leg, and tossed him clear of the fire. Then he rescued the other one.

Then Jack stood alone for a moment in the burnt straw and

batted at his clothes, which were still fuming. His eyebrows were singed and his cowboy hat continued to smoke—until the same prop man, who had retreated to safety during the high life explosion, suddenly reappeared and dumped five gallons of ice water over the burning hat, head, clothes, and boy.

Those twenty star javelinas did not especially care to be rounded up again by Wendell, assisted by wet black Jack. So the process took some time, and the afternoon waned, but the drama class stayed. And then, when the herd reassembled at the top of the hill in the propped-up pen amidst the ashes of their beloved box, those pigs were good and pissed. So when the prop man finally dropped the dummy into their midst, they ripped poor old fake Johnny Saxon to shreds in no time at all. Meanwhile, the director got lots of smoke-free shots.

Soon afterward, Jack noticed the drama students slowly and reluctantly climbing on their bus. Clearly the show was over, and the other onlookers melted away too. As the sun went down over Cochise County, Jack, Wendell, and a livestock trailer full of javelinas headed thankfully back to their native habitat.

But in the history of Hollywood that's the movie with no name. Nor did it leave a trace on TV, not on *Bonanza*, *Gunsmoke*, *The Lone Ranger*, or *The High Chaparral*—not even *F Troop*. Nor among the many thousands of totally forgotten movies and TV shows. Nowhere. Because it never came out. It was unaired.

As the years went by, Westerns continued to be made in Cochise County and elsewhere, and Jack and Wendell even played bit parts in one or two of them. But there weren't as many as before, and there was a change in the air. Even though these films were shot in Technicolor instead of black and white, all their tones seemed darker. Nothing was ever simple. The good guys and the bad guys took to switching places, and eventually, if there was no good at all anymore, it didn't matter.

Did something go haywire? Or was change inevitable? As with a random butterfly flutter, results are unpredictable and they take time to figure out. Meanwhile, real ranch life jogged along. Fifty years flew off the calendar. In the 1990s Wendell joined the riders in the sky and Jack inherited the ranch, where bandidos now sneak through the bushes with drug loads on their backs, and the horses are blasé about the sounds of cell phones.

Often, after he sells his cattle by video auction, Jack sits back and plays with the TV, where sometimes he's caught some very strange fish. Once he learned that long ago a giant meteor killed off the dinosaurs. Kaboom. Just like that! Another time, he learned that dinosaurs laid blue eggs and had feathers, and, far from dying out, they inhabited his ranch at that very moment disguised as buzzards and tiny T-Rex roadrunners.

He's also stumbled into some shady places that carried him back to his old Western movie days, although in terms of evolution he guesses *Deadwood* might be a flock of vultures, while *Westworld* is more like a chupacabras. Sometimes he remembers how the twenty singed javelinas exploded out of the stock trailer and raced away without a backward glance, reeking to high heaven.

"Can't blame the pigs," he says to himself. "Not their fault."

And then he hears a noise outside. It's no more than a displaced pebble, yet it draws him to the window. He hears a click or two, catches a whiff of something disgusting, and he knows what it is, even before he glimpses a walking scrub brush with a long snout snuffling through the bushes behind the garbage can.

And kaboom! Something hits him.

"Yeah, there's a whole lot less Westerns nowadays," Jack says to himself. "And what's left is pretty ugly. Maybe even uglier than real life, but doesn't that kind of balance things out? And yet—"

He takes another look outside. A head rises, a dirty brown cactus/animal head. It squints its little yellow eyes in his direction, and then it shows its teeth.

After living in the West for sixty-six years Jack knows one thing for damn sure. There's a whole lot more javelinas than there used to be.

Two Desperados

Shots told the whole tale. When Elizabeth remembered that day, she always heard the shots come one by one: "Pop!" And "Pop!" And then they exploded in wild volleys.

High above the spruce trees, the Alaskan sun seemed welded to the sky, and for one fearful moment Elizabeth actually forgot what day it was. But then the date flashed into her brain and she knew that time must be flowing just as fast as usual.

"June eighth, 1990," she whispered to herself and was comforted.

But she also knew, down deep, that by the end of the day something was going to happen. Probably something bad. And yet—and yet—through all the murky dread, a scintilla of something different was gleaming, a stubborn little flicker of mischief.

"Get going!" Kurt yelled through the half-built cabin and fired off another volley.

"Nails," Elizabeth told herself. "They're only nails."

Blood thumped in her ears as she raised her hammer. Not that she really needed a nail gun, but Kurt always grabbed it away.

"Gotta get the last roof truss up by dark," he said, pointing to the row of huge wooden triangles that still lay on the ground.

"Really?" she said.

How many times had they repeated this dumb dialogue? She'd begun to wonder if he was deaf, or demented. Prefabricated roof trusses supposedly saved time and money, but a construction crew usually installed them, possibly with mechanical aid, not a man and a woman at each other's throats. Bit by bit a new and even hotter relationship had replaced the one they used to have.

"Summer's short." More shots. "We gotta start roofing by dark." He narrowed his eyes at her. "I told you to take off that ring."

Safety rules, from someone who flouted them himself.

"I can't. It's stuck because my finger's swollen. And besides, my father gave it to me."

"You! Family diamonds! Silver spoons!"

"It's just a Victorian mourning ring."

"Just a *morning* ring!" Kurt mimicked her.

"It's a memorial. Years ago somebody died, I really don't know who."

And yet the enormous company of the dead constantly embraced more and more people whom she did know. Almost enough for a reunion or a club, she thought. The Memory Club. . . . But quarrels would soon break out, she feared, for so many of her lost souls were square pegs, lone wolves, and utterly unclubbable. Not of course dear Papa, who was probably already a member of several. Perhaps he had joined the Truly Historical Society. Those meetings would be enthralling, particularly if members were required to tell the truth. And then—what about the dogs? So many dogs! Would they have their own eternal park stocked with immortal jackrabbits, or would they be eternally underfoot? She looked forward very much to the dog reunions.

"And it's not a diamond," she said out loud.

At the base of her left ring finger, two tiny golden hands clasped a black enamel heart about the size of a Valentine candy, but instead of saying "Kiss Me," it was set with a pale yellow gem.

"My father said it was a topaz."

"Don't expect any kind of ring from *me*."

She felt another glorious spark. "Don't give me one!"

It was a tedious, testy job to raise and place the tresses, with Kurt up on the scaffolding operating a pulley and Elizabeth lifting and balancing from below. Each triangle added structural strength, but although they were heavy the trusses were also floppy. Truss after truss must first be braced and then nailed securely into place, and Elizabeth knew very well that Kurt was racing and cutting corners. Far-north darkness, such as it was, came late in the summer months but even so they were not going to finish before sunset.

"Listen," she said. "Swann will help us."

Their nearest neighbor lived two miles away. This far out in the woods, there was no telephone service.

"Why don't I go and get him? It's time to make up," she added unwisely.

They hadn't laid eyes on him for a month, not since he and Kurt quarreled over the location of a mailbox. Swann was a youngish middle-aged man who'd lived in Alaska many years longer than they had, so he was a real sourdough, in the local lingo, not a wannabe from the lower 48. He too had built his own house, and out of male rivalry (or jealousy, but why?) Kurt took an instant dislike to him. Spare and silent, Swann lived alone with his dogs when he wasn't working as a hunting or fishing guide, which was probably what he was doing now. Still, she took a few steps toward the pickup truck before Kurt blocked her. Of course, she thought sarcastically, Nail Gunner keeps the keys. How did she ever get into this mess? When did it stop being fun and start being—what? He gave her a sudden shove and she staggered. She was not afraid, not really. Her spark of mischief flared up brightly, then faded.

"Don't you go near him. You're not going anywhere."

"Kurt, I'm tired."

"You will do it. We're going to get those trusses up by dark."

So they tackled another one. Slowly the apex of the wooden triangle rose till it was vertical, and then it wavered. Back, forth, yes, no, it teetered, yes, no . . .

"No!" Kurt howled.

She was staring at him.

Wolf head, she thought, *no no no no*, and it was not because her arms were numb that she allowed the truss to slip away from her. It was because her head suddenly filled with boiling champagne. Kurt, as she now plainly saw, was not *it*. She was free. The whole world sparkled and she almost laughed out loud.

With a terrible roar Kurt waved his arms and lost his balance. The truss tumbled backward under his weight and then, as Elizabeth watched open-mouthed, the entire roof structure toppled like a row of dominoes and took Kurt with it. In stately progression the framed walls collapsed next, and what had been the skeleton of a cabin became a woodpile.

She found Kurt half buried in lumber. One leg was twisted at an odd angle, and he was still roaring and spitting out obscenities. In a single dreamlike action she clambered over the ruin, lifted the boards that pinned him down, and stopped short at the sight of a splintered leg bone sticking through his jeans. And then came a blaze of light as his right fist smashed her left eye.

Nothingness ended; pain began. For a long moment Elizabeth sat with her face cupped in her hands, but when she uncovered her eyes, her vision was extra sharp. Everything in the clearing appeared brilliantly clear and smaller than life. The ex-cabin was a pile of Popsicle sticks. Not *it*. Not at all *it*.

She gathered herself up from the dirt and looked at Kurt, but except for the sticky stains on her own fingers, she saw very little blood. And nobody could curse like that without being at least semi-conscious. Splint? No. Shock? Maybe. Lift him? No. Swann? Yes. Swann had a satellite phone. *If* Swann was home.

She stretched out her bloody hand. "Truck keys," she said.

"In my jacket," Kurt answered in a high childish voice she'd never heard before.

She took them, tossed the jacket over his chest, turned her back, walked steadily to the truck, and then she drove away.

2.

The bus hurtled through the night, but the single woman in the back seat could not sleep. They might be dropping through endless space for all she knew. When she closed her eyes all she saw was electric confetti.

How long had she been on the road? *What day was it now?* Panic. Not again! That was exactly the sort of question doctors asked to strain out the mad from the sane. And once again, blessedly, the answer came: June twelfth, 1990. The trip from Alaska had not gone smoothly even before money ran low and compelled her to take the bus. And why, for God's sake, did her mother not pick up the phone?

"Elizabeth Ryding," she told herself sternly, "free spirit, world traveler, rolling stone, miserable failure, you must change."

But how? Even her own name seemed alien tonight. When you got well into your thirties you were supposed to know what to do, but clearly she did not.

One thing she did know: *it.* She'd always known *it* was out there. Someday she would find it, and it would be enormous. Immeasurable. Nothing flat or simple like destiny, or a tiger in the jungle. Or maybe it was. But so far she did not know.

Beyond that cold black window lay the desert, Arizona June, a fine place to bleach your bones. Sweet home. The bus swerved slightly, and a clay-colored Plains Indian chief rose up beneath a spotlight at the edge of the highway, two stories tall, with his right arm raised high, veins bulging in a gargantuan "How!" against the night sky. Behind the warrior stood a flagpole topped with the limp shreds of the Stars and Stripes, and from a billboard Elizabeth caught the words "Adult Novelties," followed by "Feed the Ostrich!" as the bus plummeted back into the night.

But this was supposed to be a wilderness! Her father had walked through here in the early days (was it 1905 or 1906?) as a little boy in overalls following a wagon. An actual covered wagon. Yes, really. She always had the oldest father of anyone she knew. Maybe she hadn't really seen the Indian. Whatever he was, he was no Native American! Maybe she was on the wrong road.

Elizabeth had spent half a lifetime away from home while living several short separate lives—great adventures, really— each featuring a place, a job, a man, and a sudden end: *Not It*. For all she knew, anything might have happened in Arizona while she was gone, anything. Now her father was dead, and her mother nowhere to be found. Had her mother changed her phone number without letting Elizabeth know? But then surely the old number wouldn't ring. And ring. And ring.

The next road sign was a green and white rectangle:

Red Rock 5

Tucson 40

So at least she'd boarded the right bus. She squashed her nose against the black window. Coyotes out there, she thought: shriekers, killers, natural-born outlaws. Bone chewers. And then a treacherous memory slithered past all her mental barricades. Among a heap of pelts—foxes, lynxes, bears, and ermine—lay a silvery wolf skin. The wolf's head was partly intact, forming a helmet, and as Elizabeth watched in creepy fascination, Kurt thrust his own head inside the wolf's. Dead paws dangled over his shoulders, live green eyes stared beneath the glassy ones, the man's face filled the wolf's mouth, and he bared his flat human teeth and thick human tongue in a snarl and then a laugh.

"You must give up men," she said to herself.

Men were a bad habit, she thought. Like drink. Like drugs. She was a sucker for anyone, wolf head or not, who could throw her over his shoulder and carry her out of a steaming room into a snowstorm. Or vice versa. But it had to stop.

3.

After making the emergency calls, Swann had followed her back to the cabin site.

"Man," was all he could say when he saw the rubble. "Man, oh man."

Kurt was still cursing, rattling along like a small engine running rough. Putt putt, thought Elizabeth. To her eyes everything still seemed crystal-clear but far, far away. Putt, punt, puck, pit, pam, pod, pell, pitch. Punch.

"C'mon, man," said Swann after a while. "Chill out."

"She tried to kill me!"

Swann looked at Elizabeth, who spread out her hands in denial. (But had she?)

"Man, oh man, oh man." Swann tapped the nearest two-by-four with the toe of his boot. "How much bracing were you using?" he asked.

After what seemed to be decades, a helicopter appeared over the treetops, triggering the M*A*S*H theme song in Elizabeth's head: "Suicide (whap) is painless, it brings on many changes (whapwhapwhap) . . ."

"Nothing—*nothing* is painless!" she burst out, grasping Swann's sleeve.

He politely removed her hand from his arm, confirming what Elizabeth had always suspected: Swann was a deerslaying monk who liked dogs better than women—and far better than he liked men. He had a point, she thought.

After they strapped Kurt down, sedated him, and stowed the mumbling bundle in the helicopter, one of the paramedics examined Elizabeth's cheek and eye. "I don't think it's broken," he said, "but come along and get it looked at."

"No thanks," she said, "I'll drive."

She would leave the pickup at the Anchorage airport, she thought, and in defiance of the innocent Alaskan habit of leaving car keys in the ignition, she would send them back, plastered with plenty of stamps, to the mailbox of contention. If he never checked it, that was his own fault.

4.

At last the bus rumbled into the semi-bright lights of Tucson.

"A" Mountain still rose short and squat in the west, a dependable landmark, thank goodness, but Elizabeth saw that since her last visit the old downtown streets had grown very seedy, and where was the Pioneer Hotel, where she'd gone for chicken croquettes as a child and dances as a teenager?

Just for an instant she felt her date's cheek, satiny and hot beneath the prickles of his young beard; the gardenia on her shoulder had been abraded from cream to brown against his wool sports coat. They tried to escape from the ballroom down a back stairwell, where they triggered an alarm and were immediately captured by a chaperon, a fat angry judge. The boy was embarrassed. What was his name? Fletcher . . . Fraser? Didn't he go to Vietnam? Did he come back?

"But I *love* men," she thought in dismay.

She liked the sheer bulk of them, especially their salty bare shoulders. She often enjoyed their displays of unaccountable confidence and muscular strength. When men were at their best it was like swimming with dolphins. Even Kurt was fine, she thought, till he put on his clothes and began to build a house. Why did things fall apart? Why was it so often a choice between brutes and worms? Why must they butt stupidly along, steer by dead reckoning, jockey for position, and endlessly, endlessly bash things?

And how could the Pioneer Hotel be gone? Then she remembered the fire that broke out one winter night when she was away at college. Elizabeth's mother had shuddered as she described the scene. Sleepers were trapped, she said. Bodies fell through the smoke. And the Pioneer died with them, dust and ashes, dead and done with . . . yet somehow, for whatever reason, she, Elizabeth, was still here, swimming with ghosts.

At the Greyhound station the dark silhouettes slumped in the bus seats arose and turned into tired, scruffy plodders. Elizabeth shouldered her pack and followed them, stepping from the bus into familiar air at blood temperature. Skin remembers, she thought. On summer nights like this, she'd climbed out her bedroom window to ride daringly up and down Speedway all evening with a boyfriend and a thousand other teenagers. A serial killer haunted the drive-ins too, the Pied Piper of Tucson, short, pimply, teetering on the crushed cans inside his homemade elevator shoes, posing as a teenager and preying on young girls just like her. She knew a boy from another school who'd sat behind one of those dead girls in English class. The Pied Piper buried them in shallow graves in the desert, but later, in prison, he took to writing poetry, changed his name from Schmidt to Lamb, and eventually was murdered himself.

Every other human being in the bus station seemed to be either deformed or drunk and staring at her.

"My family should be here," Elizabeth thought. There they should stand, their lips smiling and their arms reaching out. "No," she whispered. "Papa's dead. And my brother, oh my brother. And where is Mother?"

Again she dialed the old home number, the one she never forgot, and once more listened to it ring. Her mother had always refused to have an answering machine.

"No Loitering," warned a sign. A poster advertised half a dozen missing children, and above the greasy pay phone a clock declared that it was one in the morning. Elizabeth lowered herself into a hard, cold plastic seat and joined the loiterers, who smelled like zoo animals; she wondered if she did too.

Four hours to daylight, she calculated in desperation. She couldn't stay there.

Money was a definite problem. Her bank balance was down to a few dollars, and travel on top of construction expenses had exhausted her credit cards. Then she glimpsed the single taxi parked outside. Covertly she counted what cash remained in her wallet: four dollars and odd change, not nearly enough for a ride to her mother's house, but now a different idea had come to her. Any port in a storm, she thought.

"How much is the fare to St. Mary's Hospital?"

The cabby raised an oversized bristly white head from the steering wheel where he was dozing. He had a complexion like ham rind. "About five dollars. Why? You sick?"

"No. Actually I want to go to Quarry Road, near the hospital."

"I know where it is," he said grudgingly.

"Not far," she suggested.

No answer. But Elizabeth opened the door and got in anyway.

Then came a grunt: "Going home?"

"'Home is where, when you have to go there, they have to take you in.'"

The words hopped out smartly like crickets from a dank cupboard. She hadn't even known they were there. In response the driver cranked down his window, hawked, and spat. Well, she thought, it *was* a sappy thing to say and most likely untrue. At the top of the big black hill, a large pale letter A luminesced in the night, A for Arizona, A for absolutely awful. And the taxi meter clicked past $4.00.

Abruptly, as though a switch had been thrown, bright light flooded an odd little arched structure by the side of the road. It glowed with rainbow colors and sparkled with silver glitter. Twinkling bulbs outlined the image of an enormous ice cream cone as well as the words "Frosty Sno." Elizabeth blinked and it vanished. Was it real or not? Was her sanity slipping? No such luck, you're just tired, she told herself as they trundled through a slumbering neighborhood of small adobe houses, their porches crowded with potted plants, their walls surrounded by yards of raked earth decorated with holy niches, topiary bushes, and wishing wells. A few windows still shone yellow behind their burglar bars (and *they* looked real enough). Well really, she said to herself, a phantom snow cone stand and a giant fiberglass Indian: is this the best you can do for visions? Perhaps the vision of adult novelties and ostriches, being words on signs, didn't really count, although she had to admit there was huge potential there.

"What's the street number?"

"You can't see it," said Elizabeth. "Just two stone gateposts. There! Turn there."

Grandfather's house lay uphill, half concealed by vegetation. Not a glint of light showed through the thorns.

"Expecting you?" sneered the driver.

As Elizabeth's eyes adjusted, the desert plants became portly columns, slim cylinders, floating saucers, masses of small hairbrushes, and several forty-foot upside-down parsnips studded with shriveled twigs.

"Look how the boojum trees have grown," she said to herself in amazement.

The taxi halted before a flight of rough concrete steps that led to a rock house. Behind the rock house rose the rugged tower that Grandfather had built, stone circle by stone circle, and christened the Keep. But was anybody actually living here anymore? The cab driver beat a tattoo with his fingertips on the steering wheel.

"Here." She thrust the four dollar bills and loose change into his hammy hand. "Wait. I'll get more inside."

"Hey!"

She marched up the steps and reached for the doorknocker, which was the bronze head of a bighorn sheep, smooth as an old coin, and exactly as she remembered. She knocked. No answer, so she pounded the door with her fist until at last a dog began to bark inside, basso profundo.

"A *big* dog," she whispered to herself. Somehow she knew it was black.

At last a light came on and the operatic dog let out a shockingly high-pitched howl, just as she noticed the taillights of the taxi jouncing down the hill.

To her relief she now recognized objects inside the house. They were smaller and shabbier than she remembered, but she could clearly recall sitting as a wiggly child in that odd armless red velvet chair. But relief was short-lived because now a truly enormous Rottweiler bounded into view, followed at a brisk scuttle by a woman wrapped in dingy white. Like the furniture, she was worn and shrunken but familiar. Her aged skin and hair looked almost as pale as her robe, and from her skinny right hand dangled a very large, very black Colt .45 pistol.

Flattening herself against the wall, Elizabeth peeked through the corner of the window. "My God, what next?" she said.

The Rottweiler barked again. The pistol wavered wildly as the old lady released the safety.

"Aunt Tinny, let me in!" Elizabeth cried, and then luckily ducked.

The bullet drilled a neat circle through the window glass, barely cracking the rest, and with a sound like the crinkle of a candy wrapper disappeared into the night. The dog went mad. Elizabeth leaped off the porch and straight into a mass of cactus spines.

"Don't shoot, Aunt Tinny. It's me, Elizabeth," she called.

The old woman approached the window and peered out suspiciously.

"I'm your niece, Elizabeth, George's daughter, and I need your help. Remember me? Can you please let me in, Aunt Tinny?"

After a long pause the old woman shakily lowered her pistol.

"Sit, Faust," she commanded the dog. Then she addressed the window. "I am *not* an ant. Ants are social insects of the family *Formicidae*. If you are who you say you are, I am your *Ahnt* Clementina Ryding. My niece should pronounce the Queen's English properly, and if you really are she, I'll thank you to remember it in future. Incidentally, I have always hated the name 'Tinny.' Your father found it amusing but I do not. Now come out of there and let me see you."

Elizabeth crept into the edge of the light.

"You are not here. You are in Alaska with some dreadful man or other."

"I'm back, Aunt Tinny, and I need a place to spend the night. If you'll let me, I'll sleep on the porch."

"*What* happened to your face?"

"A construction accident." Each time she uttered the words, they seemed a little bit truer.

"A what? Why don't you stay with your mother?"

"I don't know where she is. She doesn't answer her phone."

"Ha!" said Aunt Tinny contemptuously. "I know! She unplugs it. Well, I don't suppose you can sleep on the porch. That would look very odd. And I regret to say that the neighborhood is becoming rather unsafe."

Yes, thought Elizabeth, *it is!*

"So you'd better come in, though it's two in the morning and I am very cross about all of this. The bedrooms are occupied," she went on grandly, preceding Elizabeth past two closed doors to the end of the hall, which smelled like mothballs.

Occupied by whom, Elizabeth wondered, or what?

"So you will sleep in the study. Stay, Faust!"

Unlike the front rooms, the study looked unfamiliar, so Elizabeth guessed that she had not been allowed there as a child. It was jammed with draped furniture, knickknacks, books, and boxes, and it felt as tight as an overcrowded elevator, but from some dark nook Aunt Tinny dragged out a settee. Dropping her backpack, Elizabeth began to extract the cactus spines from her fingers with her teeth. Then she caught sight of a beige gentleman with mutton-chop whiskers and long wavy hair, hanging on the wall.

"Who's that?" she asked.

He tossed her a quizzical glance over his shoulder, almost

winking one of his blank eyes. He was quite sprightly for a plaster bust, looking as though he'd popped through the wall in a madcap moment but might vanish in another. She had never seen him before.

"That is Godfrey the Artist."

"The Artist? Is there another Godfrey?"

"*Seven Godfreys in a row*," chanted Aunt Tinny, seemingly reciting a rhyme or riddle, or perhaps even a spell, but instead of finishing it she let out a shriek. "No!"

Elizabeth had picked up a small brown photograph of a man and a woman.

The woman aimed a dagger at the man's heart. He brandished a six-shooter. Her large eyes never wavered from his face, where, beneath a mustache, he wore a roguish little smile. But she was quite serious.

"Who are *they*?" asked Elizabeth.

Aunt Tinny snatched it out of her hand.

"What cheek! Don't touch anything, I absolutely forbid you," she sputtered. "First thing tomorrow, you leave. Family papers! Very valuable! Victoria and Albert! Good *night*!"

And she was gone, leaving a whiff of mothballs behind her.

But the little brown image was still imprinted on Elizabeth's vision. The woman clutched the dagger so hard that her rings bulged below the thin leather of her glove. A fur cape covered her shoulders, and below her slender waist a long skirt fell in a formal arrangement of folds and swags. One triangle of bare skin peeped out between her sleeve and her glove.

A strap anchored the man's Western hat under his chin, but the brim was raked toward the sky. Not even nine or ten inches of elaborate millinery could make the woman as tall as this man she held at knifepoint. The fingers of his right hand were almost too big to grasp his Colt revolver comfortably, but with his other hand he raised an open umbrella. These two desperados were standing beneath a leafless tree in front of a heavy wooden garden gate.

"It must be a joke," Elizabeth said to herself. "Wild West . . . Buffalo Bill . . . Oh please, please let it all be a bad dream, and let me wake in a better place."

The threadbare little settee was clearly a close relative of the odd velvet chair in the living room, which boded ill for its comfort, and indeed Elizabeth soon discovered that it was lumpy and much too short for her to stretch out her legs. But she was too tired to care, and sleep felled her like a battering ram.

5.

A little while later she woke, or thought she woke, with a start. Not much time could have passed, for she was still exhausted and it was still dark except for the silvery city light that leaked through the window—just enough light to reveal the woman in white who stood beside her. But instead of a flannelette wrapper like Aunt Tinny's, this woman wore a long dress with leg-o'-mutton sleeves and lace ruffles at the throat, all topped off with a hat like a bridal bouquet. She had face of the woman in the photograph, but instead of a dagger she now carried a parasol, and she seemed older. She looked down at Elizabeth with an expression that was dreamy, wistful, and kind.

"Poor fish," she murmured. "Poor fish."

Bewildered, Elizabeth sat up just in time to see how tiny she was, no more than five feet tall, and to glimpse a string of amber beads around her neck and a little bangle on each wrist. Then she saw nothing at all except the cluttered room. But her heart was making a terrible commotion and sweat jumped out along her hairline.

"Fish?" she repeated.

The house was quiet except for the steady rumble of the evaporative cooler on the roof. So she must have dreamed the melancholy woman with the flowered hat—not surprising at all, considering the events of the last week and Aunt Tinny's level of weirdness. But before Elizabeth could fall asleep again she distinctly heard stealthy footsteps in the hall, followed by a little rattle and a metallic click. The doors were the old-fashioned kind with glass knobs and big keyholes. Could Aunt Tinny have locked her in? She got up and tried to turn the knob.

Yes, she could.

Or someone could. Or some thing.

"Well, there's always the window," Elizabeth consoled herself.

Brushing the curtains aside, she saw that the ground was just a short jump away. She tried the window latch, which opened with a creak. The old metal screen crumbled when she poked it: no barrier there. With luck and in daylight she would avoid landing in a cactus, and then she would find her mother, get a job, and give up men. There! She had a plan. Almost like a normal adult person.

But she was still certain that something had waked her, and that she had seen the woman in the photograph. More than seen! Air had moved. Words had been spoken. And as she stood in the gray dark, absently gnawing at the tiny cactus spines that still pricked her fingers, Elizabeth caught a glimpse of the mourning ring that her father had given her. It slipped off easily now. Slowly and thoughtfully she turned the ring over and over, watching the stone faintly scintillate, and then all of a sudden she reached out and drew the jewel down the window glass. And there, lo and behold, unless she was really asleep or she actually had lost her mind, it left a long deep scratch.

6.

In the morning Elizabeth opened her sticky eyes to heat, light, dirt, dust, and disorder. She was still wedged on the too-short settee in Aunt Tinny's junk room, where dozens of tattered envelopes addressed in sepia ink fanned across the floor. Then all of last night's impossible events came tumbling back. The window! Could any of it be true? She rose on cramped legs and stared at the frosty vertical line in the pane. So the ring must be set with a yellow diamond, not a topaz. And the door! Was she locked in? Yet now the glass knob turned smoothly and with a wary glance in both directions she stepped into the hall. But the woman in white! What about her?

Noise and smoke now issued from the kitchen, and there Elizabeth found her aunt still wearing her flannelette wrapper and bent over a pot that was boiling on the stove. The huge black dog sat at her side, and Elizabeth was glad to see that now he seemed, if not friendly, neutral.

"Aunt Tinny," she said.

"Ahnt," snapped the old woman without turning around.

"Did you come into my room last night? Did you call me a fish and lock the door?"

That got her.

"Certainly not! Don't talk nonsense."

"Someone did. She had a lace parasol and a flowered hat and called me 'poor fish.' Kindly, you know, not meanly."

Aunt Tinny's face froze. Her old skin looked more like crepe paper than ever.

"And then somebody locked my door. I couldn't get out."

At first the pale lips moved soundlessly, but at last a few words came out.

"Here you are, aren't you?"

"In the morning," said Elizabeth, "it was unlocked."

"You were dreaming," her aunt said flatly and turned back to the stove.

Elizabeth started to protest—that window glass was definitely scratched, she told herself, which must mean something—but instead she said, "May I use your phone? I'm worried about my mother."

"I just called her. No answer."

And Elizabeth got the same result. Her heart sank. Aunt Tinny fished a single egg from her pot and turned toward the kitchen table.

"Sit down," she said, giving the egg a sharp smack. It turned out to be hard-boiled. Then she shelled it, cut it scrupulously in half, and divided it between two small plates. "Only one egg in the house," she explained. She poured out two cups of tea as brown as kelp and added unexpectedly, "I expect Aurelia has just disconnected the phone."

In spite of everything, Elizabeth was touched.

"Mother always used to unplug it when she practiced," she said.

How many thousands of nights, she wondered, had she fallen asleep to the faint sweet voice of her mother's violin? The kelp tea, she discovered, was very much stewed, possibly for days.

"The milk is sour," announced Aunt Tinny with a kind of grim satisfaction. "Toast?"

A blackened silver rack contained three burnt heels of bread—ah, the source of the smoke, thought Elizabeth. She slipped one under the table to the black dog, and both he and her aunt crunched loudly.

"After breakfast," Aunt Tinny said, "I shall take you home."

Elizabeth's thanks were heartfelt.

"Would you mind stopping by the Greyhound station? My trunk is still there."

"Oh very well," said her aunt, cross again.

Elizabeth wondered if Aunt Tinny wore flannelette all day long, but soon she reappeared in a droopy old-lady camouflage garment and lace-up ankle boots.

"Come along, come along," she called. "No, Faust, you stay here."

He bared his teeth slightly at Elizabeth. Dogs don't smile, she thought, or do they? Passing the fresh hole in the front window, they made their way outside. The little car parked at an odd angle beside the Keep was exactly the color of guacamole.

"Good Lord! It's a Gremlin!" exclaimed Elizabeth.

Aunt Tinny bristled. "Why shouldn't it be?"

"I just haven't seen a Gremlin for ages, that's all."

Elizabeth glanced upward at the stone tower, which stood comfortably unchanged since her childhood. Inside the Keep there were many mysterious boxes, and down the center there was a circular staircase three stories high. No railings at all. Such fun for a child to climb on! And there were marvelous slits in the outer walls, just right for peeking or shooting arrows through. All at once, to her great surprise, she thought she caught a movement at one of the narrow windows.

"What—" she began and then thought better of it. You are in a boat, she told herself, which definitely should not be rocked. Sail on.

Aunt Tinny tramped on the accelerator and the Gremlin leaped down the hill. Elizabeth fumbled for a seatbelt but found only half of one.

"What did she look like?" Aunt Tinny demanded abruptly.

"Who?"

"The woman in white."

"Oh, a very nice face. Dreamy. Gentle. She was little, with big puffy sleeves. She wore two narrow gold bangle bracelets.

And her hat was fantastic, all roses and ribbons, with maybe a bird or a pineapple or two, and almost as big as she was, like the hat in the photograph."

"What photograph?"

"The one you took away last night. In fact, she *was* the woman in that picture, just a bit older."

The Gremlin grazed a passing garbage truck.

"Aunt Tinny! Shouldn't you st——"

"It was just a kiss," hissed her aunt, and accelerated.

7.

By daylight the bus station seemed utterly humdrum, not ominous at all, and beneath a yellow beach umbrella in an adjacent vacant lot, something unusual was going on. The red sand was riddled with trenches and burrows, while shovels, buckets, and wire screens were being operated by a small crew of perspiring workers.

"It's an archaeological dig!" Elizabeth exclaimed as she crawled from the car.

One of the diggers turned and grinned.

"Pre-Columbian?" she asked.

He laughed and shook his head. He was an unusually tall man, but dark glasses and a broad-brimmed straw hat largely obscured his face.

"Privies," he said.

"No!"

"Historic privies."

"Oh, I see. Of course." And then she added: "I worked on a dig once, in Israel."

"Really? Where in Israel?"

"A place called Tell Dan in the Galilee Panhandle."

"I've heard of it," he said.

"It's a very interesting site, a city mentioned in the Bible.

But what we found that summer was pretty dull stuff, mostly Hellenistic."

"Nothing's duller than Hellenistic," he agreed. "Not even privies."

Was he serious? He couldn't be. A good trash midden was caviar to an archaeologist, she knew.

"Come on," grumbled Aunt Tinny, so Elizabeth half-smiled, shrugged, and followed.

The trunk had somehow gained weight since she'd furiously heaved it into the back of Kurt's pickup truck in Alaska. Elizabeth managed to drag it to the door of the bus station and stopped to rest.

"Aunt Tinny, I don't suppose you could—"

"Ahnt!" corrected Aunt Tinny in a belligerent tone.

"No, of course you couldn't. Never mind."

Avoiding the stares of the archaeologists, Elizabeth finally lugged and banged her burden up to the Gremlin. But then to her great distress the ugly old thing proved to be too large to shove through either the hatchback or the doors. And by now the intensity of both light and heat was rising. It promised to be an extremely hot June day, the kind of day when the temperature exceeded 110 degrees and the hot air hummed. She sat down hard on the trunk and closed her eyes.

"Can I help?"

She opened them. The speaker was the tall man in the straw hat, and others in the crew were also looking her way. Then, somewhere deep in the dark labyrinth behind her eyes a cork popped, and even though she knew she was going to regret them later, words came fizzing out.

"I was building a cabin in Alaska and the whole damn thing fell down and my boyfriend hit me in the face and said I tried to kill him and maybe I did so I left him in the helicopter and came home to Arizona which took forever and I'm completely broke and must, must do better or I'll never find *it* in all my life, never, never, and I'm giving up men as a start but I can't find my mother who's not answering her phone so I went to my aunt—this is my aunt—excuse me, my ahnt—and she just wants to get rid of me, and then I saw a ghost, and I don't believe in ghosts but I'm afraid I really did, and now *this*!"

After a moment of silence, the tall man remarked, "That's hard to believe."

"What part?"

"Houses don't just fall down," he said calmly.

"If they're badly built by stupid maniacs they do!"

"What if we tied the trunk on the roof?" said the tall man.

He produced a coil of rope, other people came over to help, and by the time the impromptu team had lashed the trunk to the top of the Gremlin, a certain camaraderie was developing, and she'd perceived that the tall man was in charge of the dig.

Suddenly, he turned to her. "And what did you do at Tell Dan?"

"Oh, I dug. And I screened, and sorted, and took photographs and made sketches." And fended off that lascivious priest, she thought, who was always trying to get inside my tent.

"If you bring my rope back," he said, "you can work here. I'm short-handed."

"Oh! I would if I could, but I can't afford to volunteer."

"I'll pay."

"But I don't even know your name," she blurted.

"I'm Virgil." She found herself shaking a remarkably hard and dirty hand, like a baked clay tablet.

"I'm Elizabeth."

"My bite is worse than my bark, Elizabeth. I won't pay you much."

Now she was speechless. *Don't be an idiot*, she warned

herself, *this is exactly how you get yourself in trouble.* Aunt Tinny impatiently honked her horn.

"Think about it," he said.

Almost before Elizabeth could leap inside and shut the car door, her aunt launched the Gremlin backward across the parking lot.

"I don't want to get rid of you," she said sulkily. "I just wish you'd go somewhere else."

"Amen!" cried Elizabeth and grabbed instinctively for the missing seatbelt.

Ghosts—privies. Privies—ghosts. The more she considered them, the more they seemed to fit together, and the more perfectly they seemed to fit her fate in life. If she survived this trip, that is. Without warning the yellow-green car veered left against the two lanes of traffic speeding along Broadway at 50 miles per hour, and somehow arrived in one piece on Plumer Avenue, where Elizabeth finally opened her eyes. She was still alive. This cannot be *it*, she thought. *I can't die now. It's not allowed. I have things to do.*

"Slow down, Aunt Tinny," she begged. "Please!"

8.

Glancing lightly off the curb, the Gremlin finally ground to a halt in front of 2216 East Fourth Street, which like most of its neighbors was a modest bungalow built in the 1920s. There was no car in the driveway, and behind two flaky pink stucco pillars and a shallow porch, the front window blinds were down, which gave the house the appearance of having closed its eyes. Elizabeth knew immediately that nobody was home, and she felt a fresh stab of the same terror that had gripped her while they careened across Broadway. This was the right neighborhood, but the well-known rooflines, uneven sidewalks, and rows of palm and orange trees all seemed to stand in a green tornado light. Something was wrong.

Numbly she headed toward the front door. The perennially wretched Bermuda grass was gone, she noted—oh, how she and her brother had hated to mow it! They were not a lawn-growing family or, in truth, a gardening one. Apparently her mother had finally thrown in the towel, or trowel, and converted the front yard from dry grass to rocks and native plants, but today even the gravel looked sullen, thirsty, and abandoned. Several sunburned advertising flyers had been stuffed into the crack between front door and jamb. As she heard Aunt Tinny's hesitant steps coming up behind her, Elizabeth forced herself ring the doorbell.

High note, low note. Same old chime, but no answer. She really hadn't expected it. What now? Would she discover a comfortable explanation, more problems, or some unspeakable horror?

"Don't you have a key?"

"Somewhere," said Elizabeth absently.

She groped along the rough underside of the porch railing until she found the extra key in the same hiding place as ever. But before she could insert it in the lock, a series of piercing cries erupted next door.

"Lisa Bet! Lisa Bet! Honey! Is it you? Oh my God! ¡Qué milagro!"

A stout woman with improbably maroon hair came scuttling awkwardly toward them, stopping every few steps to kick the gravel out of her rubber flip-flops. By the time she reached the porch she was out of breath.

"Lisa Bet!" she gasped.

"Hello, Mrs. Murrieta."

Even an aggressive kisser like Mrs. Murrieta kept her distance from Aunt Tinny.

"Honey, it's been so long!"

"Two years. Do you know where my mother is, Mrs. Murrieta?"

"Don't even bother," said Mrs. Murrieta, gesturing dramatically at the house key. "Mami's not there."

"Where is she? Is she all right?"

"Honey," said Mrs. Murrieta, "I don't know. She asked me to watch the house when she left with that man, and she's been gone for months now."

"Man?"

"Yes, honey." Mrs. Murrieta leaned close, staring avidly at Elizabeth's bruises, and Elizabeth involuntarily took a step back. "You'll never believe this, honey, but his name was—Hiawatha!"

"Hiawatha!" exclaimed Aunt Tinny.

"I swear it on my mother's grave. Hi-a-wa-tha. He came in March. Or maybe it was April. I forget."

"Dear God," said Elizabeth and leaned heavily against the door. She had last called home in early April to announce that she and Kurt were moving beyond telephone range, and her mother seemed as serenely melancholy as usual. "Write me letters when you can, dear," she had said, and Elizabeth had sent several. But then came all the trouble with the mailbox and the mail, and with the cabin, and with Kurt, and now June was half gone by.

"What did he look like?" demanded Aunt Tinny. "He wasn't a red Indian, was he?"

A Native American, Elizabeth shouted silently. No use saying it out loud to Aunt Tinny, of course. What *was* Hiawatha anyway, she wondered irrelevantly, besides a figment of Longfellow's imagination? Chippewa, or was it Ojibwe? Did it matter? Then it struck her that soon they might be dealing with the police, and she shivered in spite of all the heat.

Suddenly Mrs. Murrieta became coy. "Well, now, I wasn't what you might call *introduced* to him, you see."

"How old was he?" Aunt Tinny cried.

"Well, honey—"

"Please tell us what you know," said Elizabeth as politely as she could. "You must have been watching."

"Honey! How can you say such a thing? I would never do that! Well, Lisa Bet, your mami knocked on my door and said she was going away with this Mr. Hiawatha and would I watch the house for a few weeks and she'd stay in touch, but she hasn't. He wasn't a young man, honey, he was really pretty old, but then so was your papi, God rest his soul, and Mami isn't as young as she used to be herself, now is she?"

"What did he *look* like?" Aunt Tinny glared, then turned to Elizabeth. "Why can't she call people by their right names? Your mother's name is Aurelia."

Mrs. Murrieta pouted, but this story was much too wonderful for her to remain either offended or silent. "He didn't look like an Indian to me. You might say he was a little bit dark-complected, honey, but he was very well dressed, coat and tie. As they got in the car, he waved at me and smiled and I waved back. Beautiful white teeth. She was driving."

"The car is gone," said Elizabeth.

"Yes, I don't know how he got here. I didn't see."

"How did she seem? Did she say where they were going, or why?"

Mrs. Murrieta pursed her lips and appeared to ransack her memory.

"Well, honey, she seemed happy. Excited, like she was having fun, you know? She gave me a key and some money and asked me to check the mail and pay the bills while she was gone, which I guess was a little funny. She never did that before. To be honest with you, Lisa Bet, she didn't seem to know when she'd be back but she did say something else—what was it? Oh, she mentioned your daddy. She said something about Papi . . . George . . . and maybe something else too, I can't remember. But I'm sure I heard that the gentleman's name was Hiawatha. How could you forget a thing like that, honey?"

"Let us go inside," Aunt Tinny urged.

So Elizabeth tried to unlock the door, which resisted at first because a dune of envelopes and catalogues had accumulated on the floor below the mail slot. The three women sidestepped this slippery obstacle and entered the living room, which was dim and stiflingly hot.

"I thought you were checking the mail," said Elizabeth. On top of the heap she could see several bills addressed to Aurelia Ryding and stamped overdue.

Mrs. Murrieta burst into tears. "*Ay Dios mío,*" she cried. "Just hire a hit man and kill me now, honey! Kill me now!"

"Pull yourself together, woman!" barked Aunt Tinny.

"Oh, Mrs. Murrieta." There was no use in blaming her, Elizabeth knew. "Tony got the money from you, didn't he?"

The sobs grew more tempestuous. Her son Tony was an off-and-on hairdresser and a dyed-in-the-wool black sheep.

"I'm going to have one of my spells," sobbed Mrs. Murrieta.

"Bother!" said Aunt Tinny. "Go outside, then, where it's cooler."

Elizabeth flicked a light switch and discovered that the electricity was off. Except for the eruption of mail, the living room was tidy, although dust had dulled the sheen of the baby grand piano. Just as he had for many years, George Ryding, aged three, gazed down from a large photograph in a gilt frame. To his daughter, little George had always seemed a terribly sober tot, but he was nicely hand-colored: white lawn ruffles, blue ribbons, round blue eyes, and golden tresses that brushed his shoulders and matched his frame.

Half-stupefied by dread, Elizabeth moved from room to room with Aunt Tinny nipping at her heels while Mrs. Murrieta sniffed and gulped and blew her nose in the living room. They found no pools of blood or ghastly mummies, and nothing in the house appeared out of order. Candles had sagged into curious shapes in the dining room, but when Elizabeth reached the kitchen she found that the scanty amount of food in the refrigerator was still cool. So the power cut was recent. In her mother's bedroom a dresser drawer gaped slightly open and a cupboard door was ajar. There was no sign of her purse, and a suitcase was also missing from its usual place. It was only when Elizabeth opened the door to the study that she came upon the first real signs of disorder. Brittle old boxes of papers and photographs had been unpacked and their contents scattered, and file folders had been dumped across the desk. In the middle of the floor stood a black metal box about the size of a small doghouse, and its heavy door hung wide open.

"The iron box," whispered Aunt Tinny.

Elizabeth had never noticed it before among all her father's funny old possessions. Perhaps he had kept it with other overflow paraphernalia in the Keep. What she did recognize was the little sepia photograph that lay inside it.

Once more the two desperados posed in the leafless garden and pretended to kill each other.

"Family papers!"

As though she had sighted a heap of gold doubloons, Aunt Tinny lunged toward the door, but Elizabeth managed to close it in her face.

"Not now," she said firmly. If these had been her father's papers, now they belonged to his heirs, and she discovered that she was feeling a small twinge of possessiveness herself. Not that she expected to find any real valuables—but then she remembered the mourning ring.

Her old bedroom had become a music room where her mother practiced and gave lessons. Elizabeth strode straight to the closet.

"Her violin is gone!"

"Then what is that?" asked Aunt Tinny, pointing at a couple of battered black cases.

"Backups. For outdoor gigs, to lend to kids . . ."

Her best violin was gone. What did this mean? Elizabeth struggled to think. Was it theft? Her mother's prized instrument was by far the most costly item in the house, worth at least twenty Gremlins, she calculated, or more, because you'd probably have to pay a junkyard to take that car. For as long as Elizabeth could remember, her mother had never let her violin out of her sight or, if possible, her touch, unless the instrument was locked up.

Mrs. Murrieta suddenly appeared in the doorway.

"Oh, honey, I feel so bad," she lamented. "I'm going to hire a hit man myself!"

"But what would you pay him with?" said Elizabeth. "Just tell me please, Mrs. Murrieta, do you remember if my mother took her violin with her? Did she have it in her hand?"

"*That* was the thing I couldn't remember, honey, but I came to tell you that I just remembered it," said Mrs. Murrieta, cheering up. "Music."

"Music?"

"She said it was about music. Why she was going."

"Music?" repeated Elizabeth. "But did she have her violin?"

"Oh yes, honey. Doesn't she always, when she's going out somewhere to play? How many times have I watched her go? And so did he, that Mr. Hiawatha. He had a violin too."

"Really?" said Elizabeth, more stunned than ever. Was he simply a fellow musician or a string-playing Pied Piper concealing the most hideous of intentions? And why, she wondered, did they leave for an indefinite time? That didn't sound like a single performance.

"I know a violin case when I see it, honey."

"Ha!" said Aunt Tinny. Then she began to teeter and Mrs. Murrieta shoved her none too gently into the nearest chair.

"Terribly stuffy in here," said Aunt Tinny with less than her usual bite.

They found the air cooler outside, especially in the shade, but Mrs. Murrieta's broad face still glistened with sweat and Aunt Tinny was visibly droopy. Both looked to Elizabeth for direction, and the way forward immediately became clear. She pushed aside the terror and the doubt.

"Wait here," she said, pointing at a pair of cobwebby porch chairs. "Please? I'm going to pack a few things, and then, I'm sorry, Aunt, I mean Ahnt, Tinny, I know how you feel about me, but with no water or power here, I'm afraid I must—"

"I hope you will stay with me as long as you wish," said her aunt in a majestic tone. "And you may call me whatever you please."

Elizabeth was almost too staggered to thank her coherently. In response the old woman inclined her head and requested a glass of water.

"Yes, yes, of course."

Nothing but explosions of air flowed from the faucets, but Elizabeth did find a bottle of water in the refrigerator and snatched it out along with everything else. Unfortunately, since the half egg and burnt toast had long since worn off and she was beginning to feel very hungry, her mother's kitchen was nearly as bare as Aunt Tinny's, except for some canned goods and staples. Elizabeth piled these into shopping bags along with at least twenty pounds of mail, which seemed to be mostly junk.

"And now," she said to Aunt Tinny, when the car was packed, "you really must let me drive. In fact I insist."

"Oh, very well," said her aunt with a sniff.

As Elizabeth attempted to fire up the reluctant Gremlin, Mrs. Murrieta, who had been hovering at a slight distance, rushed to tap the driver's window. Perhaps she'd remembered something else, something useful?

"Lisa Bet!" she panted. "You really should put a little makeup on your face. Then whatever happened to you won't show at all, honey, not a bit. I'll lend you some."

"Oh," said Elizabeth. "I'm fine. But thanks all the same."

Mrs. Murrieta stepped back and flapped a disappointed hand at them.

So Elizabeth relented. Leaning out the window, she called, "It was just a construction accident! Nothing serious. See you soon!"

Mrs. Murrieta brightened, flapped her hand again, and watched intently till the car turned left from Fourth Street onto Plumer and disappeared from sight.

9.

Elizabeth arranged an assortment of food on Aunt Tinny's kitchen table: crackers, dried apricots, peppermint candies, a jar of peanuts, and a can of tuna.

"Grub first," she said.

"Then ethics," replied Aunt Tinny, much to her niece's surprise, until she recalled that this was her father's half-sister, and even a closer relative if you considered that their mothers were sisters, so the old grub joke had probably been handed down in the family. Sayings were a heritage: little catchwords, private jokes. It was almost a secret code. When and if she and Aunt Tinny ever sat down to lettuce together, perhaps the lettuce joke would come up, and even, if appropriate, the cauliflower one.

"Or," Elizabeth went on, "is it grub first, then police?"

"I shall take some tunny fish," said her aunt, declining to answer the question.

"Certainly. Very nutritious. But *is* she a missing person? She's an adult, after all. Where's the can opener?"

They ate in silence until the fish was gone, and then they started in on the nuts and crackers. A most appropriate menu, Elizabeth remarked to herself.

"I think I'll go through the mail next," she said out loud. "Maybe I'll find some kind of clue there."

"Down, Faust," murmured her aunt.

Elizabeth let fall a cracker, and the black head vanished beneath the table.

"Soon we must go grocery shopping," she said brightly. Even her aunt must live on something, she reasoned. But Aunt Tinny merely looked cagy and continued to chew. Surely she had some source of income? Or was she in the process of crazily wasting away? Faust also seemed hungry, and given his size and his teeth, that was a serious matter.

"Have you called her friends?" asked Aunt Tinny, suddenly practical.

"Well, no. That's next. I didn't have their phone numbers while I was traveling, and I didn't want to cause a fuss over nothing. But now I will."

They chewed diligently on the dry apricots.

"When did you see her last?" asked Elizabeth.

Aunt Tinny looked thoughtful. "At the final symphony of the season, I think."

"I talked to her about the same time. Early April, right?"

Her aunt nodded. "*Ode to Joy*," she said gloomily.

"The problem with Mrs. Murrieta is that she watches all day long but she doesn't really see what's going on, so I don't know how much to believe."

"Afterwards we had tea and cake."

"And how was she?"

"She seemed fine. She said you were building a house."

"Well, I was."

"Why don't you ever *marry* these men?"

"Why didn't *you?*"

In the dead silence that followed, Elizabeth slipped Faust another cracker. Then she offered a conciliatory peppermint to her aunt, who surprised Elizabeth first by accepting it, and even more by what she said next: "We still might!"

When the scraps of this luncheon were swept away, Elizabeth began to sort the mail. Soon there was quite a pile of bills, and she wondered tiredly how much money the unfailingly rotten Tony had extracted from his mother; he and his father, a dour retired postman, were not on speaking terms. She wondered, too, why her mother had taken the risk of leaving Mrs. Murrieta in charge of anything at all except possibly watching the house. This seemed out of character, unless perhaps she was in a hurry, but that seemed out of character too. Except for the *Sturm und Drang* of music—and of course the temperament of other musicians—Aurelia Ryding led a tranquil, orderly life, or so it had always seemed. As Elizabeth continued to sift the few letters from the many advertisements, she worried out loud.

"If Mrs. Murrieta is telling the truth, my mother seems to have left happily and voluntarily. I do feel relieved to hear that. Or maybe I don't. Who is this Hiawatha anyway? Why would she go anywhere with him?"

Aunt Tinny, who had been staring absently at a crack in the wall, now spoke.

"Watha wouldn't hurt a fly," she said.

Elizabeth had just discovered one of her own letters to her mother, unopened, as well as a letter from her mother to herself, which had been sent in April to that infamous mailbox in Alaska but returned, stamped "Insufficient Address." She tossed them both aside and jumped to her feet.

"*Watha?*"

Avoiding her gaze, her aunt made no reply.

"Okay, Aunt Tinny," said Elizabeth, hands on hips. She waited for her aunt to snap "Ahnt!" but she did not. "Enough. No more dark hints and questions and allusions and silences. You know something. Start talking."

"Well, we always called him Watha," Aunt Tinny said at last. "Hiawatha is quite a mouthful, isn't it."

"Go on."

"I don't know what to say. My feelings are hurt."

"I apologize, but I need to know what's going on. You must understand. Please!" Not for the first time, Elizabeth wondered if her aunt's mind was sound. Perhaps she needed a guardian.

"No, it's not you. Watha should have come to *me*," said Aunt Tinny. "Not Aurelia."

"WHO IS HE?"

Elizabeth had just concluded that Aunt Tinny must indeed be insane—and was it hereditary? Could that explain the two-story Sitting Bull and the uncanny Frosty Sno stand?—when she finally spoke.

"If he is who I think he is, his name is Hiawatha Coleridge Taylor, and he and your father and I are first cousins, or we were," said Aunt Tinny with a sigh. "Our mothers were sisters. Oh, I was very fond of Watha—he was my favorite cousin. Such a kindhearted boy! And so good-looking. Of course he was very musical, as we all were. It runs in the family. Some of us sang and some of us played and some of us did both. Ah me, it's all so long ago and so, so far away. I do wish he'd come to see me! He was older than I am, you know, so he must be well over eighty now."

Elizabeth had never heard so many words at once from Aunt Tinny before. It almost made up for being shot at. And, she reflected, there must be more to know, much more.

"So," she said thoughtfully, "he—Hiawatha!—would be my first cousin once removed, times two?"

Aunt Tinny nodded.

"But he's not even part Native American?"

"Come back to the study, and I'll show you some pictures," said Aunt Tinny, and she almost smiled. Now she did not seem crazy at all.

In terms of dust and chaos, the two Ryding studies were remarkably similar. While Aunt Tinny scrabbled in boxes, Elizabeth took a cautious seat on the red settee. "But I'll never spend another night on this ghastly thing," she vowed to herself. Luckily there was a sleeping bag in her trunk, which by means of a long sweaty struggle she had transferred from the Gremlin to the house.

She thought about the archaeological dig. She must return that rope as soon as possible, for in her experience, work on digs started and finished early on broiling summer days. And what about the man named Virgil (was it his first name or his last?) Privies—ghosts. Privies? Ghosts? *No. No more mistakes. No men.* But then Elizabeth reflected that she and Aunt Tinny really needed some decent food.

"That's Watha on the right." Aunt Tinny held out a faded picture of four Edwardian children squinting in a patch of sunshine, two boys and two girls. "Next to him is his sister, Gwendolen, a very pretty girl, isn't she, and then your father, and the little one in the pinafore is me."

Elizabeth studied the children closely. "I see," she said.

"And this is their mother, Jessie, my youngest aunt."

Not beautiful but formidable, Jessie faced the world with steely eyes, a high-necked shirtwaist, and an altitudinous hat.

Don't cross Jessie, Elizabeth thought. *Oh, how I wish she were here now to help me out.*

"And here's her husband, Samuel Coleridge Taylor, their father."

"Samuel Coleridge Taylor?" said Elizabeth. "Not . . . Samuel Taylor Coleridge?"

Then she looked at the portrait. Formally dressed, Samuel Coleridge Taylor turned from his seat at the keyboard of a grand piano. It was a black and white photograph and so was he: a handsome Anglo-African about forty, smiling slightly at the camera. He had a sensitive and intellectual face.

"He was very famous," Aunt Tinny said. "He was a musician and composer who died far too young. Alas."

And she held out one more portrait.

Elizabeth gasped. This young woman's loose, wavy hair rippled past her waist and spilled on to the seat of her chair. She glanced over her shoulder with eyes that were wide-set and heavy-lidded. Her narrow face was grave. It was more of a portrait of the hair than the girl but nevertheless she was another, much younger version of the same woman who had appeared before Elizabeth in the dark the night before.

"That's Lily," said Aunt Tinny. "My aunt. Your grandmother."

Elizabeth was speechless.

"*I* never see her," Aunt Tinny added accusingly. Then she brightened. "But maybe now that *you're* here. . . . She spoke, you said?"

"Fish! She called me 'poor fish.'"

"Ah!"

What did that mean? Elizabeth waited for an explanation but her aunt was silent.

"Now really, Aunt Tinny," she finally burst out. "This is all getting a little too—"

The old lady wore a faraway expression. Although the

photographs seemed real, Elizabeth wondered again if her aunt was insane.

"Perhaps, if we're very fortunate indeed, she'll sing. She was a contralto."

"Music again!"

"Why, everything's about music, my dear," said Aunt Tinny, surprised. "Don't you know that?"

10.

Just as Elizabeth had guessed, by two o'clock in the afternoon the archaeological dig lay tidy and deserted. She climbed out of the Gremlin anyhow and squelched her disappointment. Perhaps she could leave a note, she thought, and after all, Aunt Tinny did have a working telephone. She could look him up under "Virgil" perhaps. Or perhaps not. As she surveyed the dust, she reasoned that if there were privies, once there must have been houses here. Maybe adobe houses? Ah, ashes to ashes, dust to dust for sure, she thought, and her heart shivered and sank. The afternoon sun was so powerful that the heat seemed to reverberate like a gong. It was odd to feel both hot and desolated at once, though surely tragedy was just as likely to strike at 110 degrees as 40 below.

"You're back."

Elizabeth spun around as the man in the wide straw hat strode toward her from the direction of the bus station.

"I brought the rope," she said. "Thanks very much. I thought I'd missed you."

"Had to make a quick phone call, or else you would've."

"On the greasiest pay phone in the lower 48?"

He laughed. "That's the one!"

Suddenly, last night seemed farther away than the last century.

"Where's your aunt?"

"She likes to take a period of quiet meditation after lunch."

He chuckled and once more Elizabeth wished she could read the eyes behind the dark glasses.

"What about the ghosts?" he asked.

"Oh, they're quiet. There were some old pictures lying around in my room, and I'm beginning to think probably I just had a nightmare instead of some kind of supernatural vision. Much more likely."

Everything would be *so* much easier if that were true, she told herself, and it probably was, no matter what bizarre beliefs Aunt Tinny seemed to hold. Away from the stone house and the Keep, guarded by their thicket of thorns, none of the oddball goings-on seemed real.

"Hm," he said with a little smile. "I've always been interested in ghosts myself." He gestured toward the dig. "Plenty of them out there, you know. And did you find your mother?"

"Well, no." Her heart dipped. *Don't go into it!* Don't make a fool of yourself again!

A pair of black eyebrows arched above the black lenses of his sunglasses.

"Let's move into the shade," he said, pointing at a nearby tamarisk tree. Like all tamarisks, it was ungainly and scruffy, seemingly a normal tree fallen on bad times, but it did cast a ragged gray shadow.

"Wait!" Elizabeth blurted. "If your offer still stands, I do need a job."

"All right then," he said equably. "Minimum wage. We start at six."

They reached the shade, where he put his hands in his pockets, looked down at her, and showed no signs of moving, but somehow the silence was not uncomfortable.

Looking over his shoulder, she noticed for the first time that brilliant white cumulus clouds were building against the intense blue of the eastern sky. A gust of wind whiffed across the dig, raising a couple of small dust devils and rattling the shabby needles of the tamarisk tree. It also carried a reek of diesel exhaust as a Greyhound bus rumbled into the station. Virgil followed her gaze up to the sky.

"You know what they say."

"Who?" she asked.

"My Tohono O'odham friends: Wind Man carries Rain Man on his back, because Rain Man is blind."

"It's way too soon for the summer rains, though," Elizabeth objected. "It's only June."

"Right."

"I should go," said Elizabeth.

"What about your mother?" he said.

"I—"

"Go on."

"Oh dear, oh dear, I'm very concerned. She's gone, and her purse is gone and the car is gone and the utilities have been shut off. It's not like her. But I don't know why I'm bothering you with all of this. There must be an explanation."

"She lives alone?"

"My father died six years ago. Oh! Her violin is gone too. She's a musician."

"So. Did she go on vacation, or is she a missing person?"

"I don't know," said Elizabeth miserably. "She's an adult, after all, and she wasn't expecting me. I've checked with a few of her friends and colleagues, and so far nobody knows where she is. And I must say they don't seem worried. But—"

"But what?"

"According to the nosy neighbor next door, my mother left suddenly, months ago. With a man."

He smiled. "Well?"

"A man named Hiawatha."

He gave a shout of laughter.

"Did he come by canoe? Sorry."

"I know how it sounds," said Elizabeth, waving off his apologies. "He may actually be some sort of relative—a long-lost cousin, according to my aunt. Suddenly I'm learning things about my family that I never even suspected before."

"Tell me your name again. Elizabeth what?"

"Ryding," she said with a sigh.

"Ryding," he repeated.

"And is Virgil your first or last name?"

"Virgil Holden," he said. "Almost everybody just calls me Virgil. *Ryding*, though, Ryding is a name that rings a bell, an old Arizona name. Are you by any chance related to Godfrey Ryding, or George Ryding?"

Elizabeth hesitated, looking down at the reddish dirt under her feet. Would the connection help or hurt her with this curious man? But she'd given up men anyway, so what did it matter?

He pursued the subject. "The Rydings who came in the 1800s and did all the exploration and made the maps and lived with the Hopis and built the laboratory and the tower on the hill? The mad Rydings?"

"Well, yes," she admitted. "I'm Godfrey's granddaughter and George's daughter, but I've been away for a long time."

"Really? I hope you'll stay awhile. I want to ask you a lot of questions about the Rydings. Historic archaeology is my specialty."

Elizabeth muttered something about not knowing the answers.

"We had a good day today," he said, changing the subject. "We hit paydirt, so to speak, and that's what I was phoning about. Want to see?"

From his left pocket he pulled a plastic bag containing a dirty, hollow object slightly larger than half a walnut shell.

"Is it—pottery?"

"It's a bowl, all right, but I think it's the bowl of an opium pipe, and if we're really lucky we'll find some traces inside." He extracted another plastic bag from his right pocket. "And then there's this."

A pair of bright blue eyes stared out of his palm. The nose that accompanied them was disproportionately tiny, and the cupid's-bow mouth even more so. But the circles of hectic pink flush on the cheeks were large, suggesting illness or sunburn, for the rest of the little blonde's face was as white as eggshell or a fine teacup. She had been decapitated long ago but her face remained serene.

"The head of a china doll," Virgil said. "Bisque, to be exact."

"Wow," marveled Elizabeth. "Did she belong to an opium-smoking little girl?"

"Probably not. These came from two different privies, and most likely the pipe—if it is an opium pipe—belonged to Chinese laborers working on the railroad, which came to Tucson in 1880. And of course the railroad tracks are still right over there, behind the trees."

"A Chinese storekeeper, perhaps."

He nodded. Life upon life, Elizabeth thought, contemplating the vacant lot again. Little lives, like ours. A spark and gone.

"Isn't it strange," she said out loud, "that a doll should last longer than a child?"

She wanted to know how objects like the pipe and the doll's head ended up in privies, and he said it was probably a combination of trash disposal and accidents.

"The trash heap of history," she said.

"Yup. Isn't it wonderful?"

Suddenly it occurred to Elizabeth that Aunt Tinny was probably awake by now and would deplore—to say the least—the joint absence of her niece and her Gremlin. So, mumbling a few words about family papers and tomorrow morning, she beat a hasty retreat.

"Good luck with the ghosts," Virgil called after her.

She could hear a gurgle of laughter in his voice, but also something serious. In turn she felt a little flicker of fear, or gusto, or both. Or perhaps of mischief. Maybe, although she knew her behavior was rash and would almost certainly lead her into trouble, as usual, yet maybe, just maybe, this choice would lead her to . . . *it?*

"Whatever happens," he shouted, "take notes!"

"Oh, I will!" she promised, and on she ran.